Comments and Reviews from Previous Books
by Anita L. Allee

Closed, Do Not Enter
Set in Jefferson City, MO area
Orphan Train & Civil War in MO, TX & LA
"I cried when I saw your book on the shelf, I knew it was
your dream."
"When will the next one be out?"
"I could not lay the book down until it was finished."
"There's only one problem, the books are too short."

Child of the Heart
Set in Old Franklin & Boonville, MO
About Teachers, students & slaves
Santa Fe Trail Boss

From two nine year olds:
"I understood the book and liked it."
"My grand daughter devoured your book."
Young Mother/teacher: "After reading the book, I stop often
and pray as the characters did."

Future Titles:
Back Country Adventure
Contemporary-Do It Yourself Witness Protection
River Run-sequel to *Child*
Who's the Boss
Colorado Homesteading-gender role exchange
Two Together
Community Saga

Yankee Spy in New Orleans

Anita L. Allee

Historical Novel

Set in Missouri
&
New Orleans

1861-1865

**Missouri Center
for the Book**

**Missouri Authors
Collection**

Copyright © 2004 by Anita L. Allee
All Rights Reserved
Cover Painting by Mary King Hayden

ISBN: 1-59196-567-5

Published in USA by Instant Publisher.com
PO Box 985, Colliersville, TN 38027

This is a work of fiction. Historic characters and events are used within the perimeters of historic fact. All other characters and events are fictitious.

Ultimate design, content and editorial accuracy of this work is the responsibility of the author.
Scripture references are paraphrased by the characters from the King James Version of the Bible

Publisher's Cataloging-in-publication

          1. Civil War history in New Orleans, LA
          2. Iron mining in Iron County, Missouri
Fiction-title

Printed in the United States of America
by
InstantPublishers.com
Contact author at: anviallee@earthlink.net

Dedicated to my daughters,
Vinita and Diann
Who give inspiration
for this and many
other areas of my life.

A special thanks to my cover
artist and friend, Mary King
Hayden who goes above and
beyond what I ask.

Message to readers:
Thank you for the inspiration you
continue to give in
reading and commenting on previous books.
May we continue our partnership as
writer and reader.

Characters: *Yankee Spy in New Orleans*

Sarah Turner aka Sarah Tourn'e - youthful woman with a vendetta

Montgomery Adkisson - Young Confederate Mercenary in New Orleans

Clem Davis - Fuqua Store clerk and Yankee Contact

Samuel Henri - "Cajun" Yankee Contact

Cleota - Negro Companion and Yankee Spy, freed slave

Gideon - physically weak New Orleans slave boy

Lawrence Asden - Lecherous Confederate businessman

Richard Turner of Turner Iron Works, Sarah's father

Daniel Roberts - payroll clerk at the Iron Works, and Sarah's fiancee

Samson and Josie - husband and wife, butler and cook at New Orleans mansion
Moses - Cleota's friend

Setting:
Beautiful antebellum mansion in New Orleans leased by Confederate sympathizer, Montgomery Adkisson, but secretly owned by Yankees.

Generals Butler, Banks, and Sharpe are historic figures from Union Civil War events.

Yankee Spy in New Orleans

Early 1861
<u>St. Louis, Missouri, Turner Iron Works</u>

Twenty-one year old Sarah Turner rubbed a tense spot in her neck. She pushed dark strands of escaped hair from her face and neck, then stretched her back against her father's huge desk chair. The petite woman raised her head from the Turner Iron Works' ledger. She looked around the lantern-lit room.

I love this office. I should get a smaller desk and chair, but I love Papa's desk and my little footrest. Papa can't even get his knees under his desk. She rubbed her hand over the worn places on the drawers. *I spend more time in his chair than he does.*

Except when we go on river expeditions, this is the best place I know. Ever since my momma died, Papa and Cleota have been my family and this has been my home.

Sarah closed her eyes. For the first time in hours, she listened to the reassuring hum of the big blast furnaces and the clang of hammers in the foundry where the workers formed cannon and other war artillery for the Union army. She lowered the wick in the desk lamp. *My lullaby. All's well.*

A shout drew her attention.

The men are noisier than usual tonight. I'm glad they can take a break, we've all worked too hard lately to fill this last contract.

"Miss Sarah, Miss Sarah!" a rough voice yelled.

In a practiced movement, she removed her feet from the bench she used under her father's desk. Despite her long skirt, she flipped her right foot into the scuffed mark she'd worn at the center of her father's second drawer from the bottom. She pushed and spun her father's chair to face the door.

A workman banged the door open, then held it when it rebounded against his arm.

"Your father's injured. Come quick!"

Accustomed to injuries and burns on the job, Sarah bounced down from the chair and opened the lid to the red box by the office door. She lifted the burn basket and let the lid fall as she whirled away.

Dread filled her heart. She stopped to look into the worker's face, "How bad is he?"

"Hurry. Come this way, I've got the door for you."

Sarah rushed out onto the walkway, "Did you send for the doctor?"

"Yes, several men went for him. You never know where he'll be at this time of—   ."

"Where's my father?"

The workman guided Sarah along with his hand on her back.

"We've got him under the lanterns on the dock."

She turned her head toward the loading area.

Breathlessly the man continued, "The payroll was coming up from the river. Three men tried to take it away from the courier. There was a struggle, your father and someone else went to help. We heard shots."

"Shots? You mean he's wounded?"

"Yes. The robbers ran when we got to Mr. Turner. It was dark, we couldn't see much."

The pair rushed to the knot of men standing on the loading dock. Sarah's attention went immediately to the downed figure of her father. She sat the basket beside him and knelt. A handful of linen bandages filled her hand.

"Papa, are you all right?"

Mr. Turner opened his eyes, "I'll be fine, but—," he hesitated, "I'm afraid for Daniel, he hasn't moved. I think he's worse than me."

"Daniel?" Sarah rose as she spoke and looked down the dock at the other two bodies lying in front of another group of men. The first, her uncle, groaned as she rose. The second body lay very still. Before she reached him, Daniel coughed, a gush of blood spurted from his chest. Sarah gathered his head into her arms and pressed the wad of linen into the gapping wound.

"Daniel, Daniel! It's me, Sarah."

She directed the men. "Get the payroll bag off his arm."

"I— I saved the payroll," Daniel gasped.

"Rest easy, the doctor is on his way." *So much blood, so much blood, how can I stop it? My hand is too small.*

She appealed to one of the gathered workmen, "Give me more of that linen. Press it here and here. Hold it tight, we've got to stop his bleeding."

"Sarah— I heard— three men say they were after money for Adkisson. They said he wasn't gonna like it if he didn't get— *war money*."

"What, Daniel, what is it? I can't hear." She placed her ear at his lips.

"I love you-ou." His voice faded away with a gasp.

The circle of men shook their heads. One gently took Sarah by the shoulders. He attempted to lift her away from Daniel's body, "He's gone, Miss Sarah."

"No! Where's the doctor. He can do something. Hurry!" Sarah was desperate, *I can't lose my fiancee now.*

"I'm sorry. We'll do what we can for your father and your uncle," the foreman laid his hand on Sarah's arm.

"Here's the doctor! Make way, make way," another workman said.

The men moved back at the voice in the rear.

The doctor knelt to place his ear on Daniel's chest, then rose to shake his head.

"Please, he's not gone, is he?" Sarah pleaded.

"My dear, he's dead." Her old friend patted her shoulder and turned toward her father. "We'll see what we can do for your father and uncle."

Moments later the doctor declared Richard Turner and his brother out of immediate danger.

Sarah's blaze of anger cleared tears from her eyes. She turned back to the body of the young man. She touched his hand and whispered, "Daniel, I'll see this man— whoever he is, punished.. He can't get away with this!"

"Sarah, come here," her father raised his hand to her.

Woodenly she moved to obey. He clasped her cold fingers in his.

"I'm sorry, Honey. We'll get the ones who did this!"

"Papa, you rest now!" Her tears ceased, she became a cold machine concentrating on her new purpose. *Adkisson's War money, whatever that means, I won't forget.*

Assignment

After months of intense and emotional nursing by Sarah and Cleota, her father remained a shell of his former vigorous self and her uncle bore the after-effects of his injuries in his painful limp.

The workers of the iron works rallied around the two men and vowed to continue work until the two recovered. All were grateful for young Daniel's sacrifice.

"He gave his life for our pay."

"Let's keep this place going for Mr. Turner and Miss Sarah!" the men shouted.

The federal government's secret police located Montgomery Adkisson in southern ports. He operated out of New Orleans where he sought to promote himself, and secondly, southern war efforts. Now that they knew his identity and activities for the new Confederate government, they wished to capitalize on this knowledge..

In an office in Washington, D.C., spychief General George H. Sharpe met with his committee. A meeting to plan further espionage strategy for the Union.

Again and again as the committee enumerated the characteristics required for their informants, Sarah Turner came into the mind of committeeman, Stewart Bland.

At first, Stewart resisted his thoughts, but then he examined his memories. *Sarah lost her fiancée to the very man we seek. Her father was injured in that robbery attempt at the foundry. I know Sarah very well, she could do this job.*

Against his own better judgment, he finally voiced his ideas to the committee.

"You may not fully appreciate my suggestion, but I know of a young woman with her freed slave companion who will fit all the criteria we've named."

"Two women, what are you thinking? You know we can't send women to New Orleans alone," another of the committee questioned.

Stewart answered, "A very young woman would a-rouse less suspicion than a man *and* she's the young woman who lost her fiancée in the foiled robbery at her father's iron foundry. She is of staunch Union people. She has a freed Negro woman as her companion."

"*Two women*, that's worse than ever," another replied.

"Think about it, we know that women are less suspect than males and runaway slaves are some of our most valuable sources of information," General Sharpe commented.

"Sarah is very small, but has traveled extensively with her father. I've seen her perform dialects since she was a small child. Her education has been unusual. Her companion being a former slave understands the system. The companion is in her later thirties and very stable. A servant would not be unusual in New Orleans," Stewart added. "They're from St. Louis, Missouri."

Another of the committee broke in, "We *have* used women for couriers, but only in more protected areas or near the borders between the Confederacy and Union-held territory. Missouri qualifies because it's a border state. But I question the sophistication of a Missourian for a mission such as this."

"We've used some females in permanent placement at listening posts. The south is being successful with women.

We've taken several prisoners," and aid reminded the committee members.

"That's what I'm afraid of, they'd be taken prisoner," General Sharpe added.

"We could place them in a home. That would not likely be a dangerous place," Stewart remarked, "And you will find these ladies as sophisticated and intelligent as any of their age."

"But how do you know those we seek will act civilized? Don't you recall, 'All's fair in love and war'?" General Sharpe commented. "This man's hirelings attempted a robbery and committed murder."

"We can't be entirely sure of their safety, but believe me, this young woman and her companion have unusual abilities and intelligence. If anyone can handle this, they can," Stewart argued.

"I'm not convinced."

"When Sarah was small, her father sometimes dressed the little girl as a boy. She was inconspicuous during his negotiations with customers. She is very self-disciplined and in her early twenties. She was her father's constant companion since the death of her mother when Sarah was a toddler. She's traveled over this country more than any of us. Her companion, Cleota, has been with Miss Sarah during much of her travel," Stewart continued with his argument. "They've lived in St. Louis, but she's traveled the Ohio, Mississippi, Missouri and Arkansas Rivers. She and her father have been present at some of the largest and most important gala affairs and industrial meetings in our land."

"I don't like it at all. If she's been everywhere, she might be recognized," General Sharpe noted.

"Now, wait a minute. Just think about it— Sarah is very small, she could pass for a youngster from the back country, which would explain her lack of some background in New Orleans. Her servant could pose as her slave. Sarah is able to imitate local dialects. I've seen her play parts from up and down the Mississippi River. She is a remarkable actress. I think you need to meet her. You could question her and see for yourself. Think about it, a very young woman would arouse less suspicion than any man we could recruit," Stewart added.

"Why would a young woman wish to take on an assignment like this? It could be dangerous and surely no women would want to leave their comfortable home and get themselves into this kind of situation," General Sharpe stated.

"Miss Sarah has a stake in this. She's a quiet abolitionist but most of all, it was her fiancée who was killed when they attempted the robbery at her father's iron works in Missouri," Stewart reminded the two. "I insist you meet the pair before you turn hands down."

"I don't think it would work."

"I guess you won't give in until we interview her," a reluctant aide stated.

"Yes, I'd like to meet such remarkable women, but don't count on this going anywhere," General Sharpe said, "If chosen they'd have to know this is a very dangerous game we're playing."

"With the loss of her fiancée, I have no doubt she realizes the seriousness of catching this scoundrel. I'll get them here as soon as I can," Stewart answered. "I've been going over in my mind a good scenario. If accepted, I propose they be slipped into New Orleans under the disguise of a misplaced orphan, amongst refugees from the outlying areas of the south, and accompanied by her black slave woman, aptly played by Cleota, her surrogate mother and long-time friend."

"Set up the meeting, but don't count on me agreeing with your call on this one. I don't like it at all," General Sharpe grew restless with the long discussion. "We need to move on to other topics."

Sarah and Cleota agreed to the planned meeting in

Virginia.

The events at home had made the two easy recruits for this proposed spy mission. Sarah's appearance served well, slight and only five foot, she looked quite young. Dressed appropriately with chest binding she could pass for a young fourteen-year-old orphan with Cleota serving as her personal slave.

Sarah prepared the foundry workers for their absence. She was in agreement with the workers as she addressed them, "You know my father and I very well, most of you have been with us since I was a child. I know your loyalty to my father. She continued, "I must be gone for a time on business for the foundry. Very soon, my father expects to run the works as usual. I'd certainly appreciate it if you could see fit to continue on here, as before. My father will come back to work full-time as soon as he's able. In the meantime, depend on David Solomon as foreman, just as you have these last few months. Thank you for all you've done to help us keep things going."

She choked and turned from them, got hold of herself and spoke her final words in a clear voice, but with her back to the men, *her family for many years*, "Thank you."

"Miss Sarah, we'll miss you," the old foreman spoke for the men.

"I'll miss you too. Take care— ," Sarah could say no more. She moved quickly away.

The men stood looking after her, several swiped at their noses. With bowed heads, they quietly turned back to their tasks. Few words were uttered.

&

Stewart Bland informed General Sharpe's aide, "I have arranged for our two ladies to meet us at a friend's home in Virginia. Our committee will meet there at seven thirty in the evening on the tenth. Miss Turner and her servant will arrive at eight. The two have agreed to answer any of your questions at that time."

On the tenth, two of the committeemen arrived together and were ushered into the home by a household servant. They were seated in the library and offered refreshments. When the servant retired, a young girl quietly passed in and out of the room assisting in their comfort. Accustomed to southern servants, neither man noted the pair.

Stewart Bland arrived with General Sharpe and hurried ahead of the servant into the library. "Thank you, that's all. Miss, you may go now."

The two committee members became impatient. "Have you made the arrangements for us to talk with the ladies about a possible assignment?"

"I certainly have."

"Were they agreeable?"

"They were," Stewart said.

"If they were accepted by all, we would still have many details and they would require months of training by our organization."

"Yes, definitely."

A light tap came on the door. Conversation ceased. The slave entered and refilled the glasses. She bowed and backed toward the door.

"Massa, will that be all?"

"Yes, thank you."

By nine the men shifted in their chairs. "Are the ladies coming?"

Stewart Bland laughed, "You should know, ladies always make gentlemen wait."

"Well I don't have all night. I need to get back to Washington. I am scheduled to leave at six in the morning on an important matter to the west," General Sharpe looked at the swinging pendulum of the mantle clock.

Stewart chuckled, "Guess I've kept you waiting long enough." He went to the door. "Miss Sarah, Cleota, you may come in now."

The men rose to welcome two ladies into the room. Only the two servants that welcomed them earlier, entered.

"Where?"

"Gentlemen, may I introduce Cleota, and— Miss Sarah Turner?"

"Huh. What do you mean?"

Stewart beamed, "These two ladies are in the roles they would take, should we allow them to serve the Union."

"Stewart, you fooled us this time, but you haven't got us yet. I have many questions," General Sharpe said.

"Ladies?" the general bowed and motioned toward chairs on the far side of the desk. "Shall we proceed?"

Sarah removed her mop cap. No longer playing a role, her demeanor changed into serious, take charge business woman.

"Please, let us proceed," she said.

Serious questioning followed with thoughtful answers.

She and Cleota convinced the three men of their qualifications for this particular mission.

General Sharpe ended his part of the interview with a warning, "If discovered you could be sentenced to death and executed."

Sarah looked into the eyes of each of the men. "Cleota and I have discussed that possibility. For our country, we're both willing to take that risk."

The men shifted.

"We wouldn't be able to acknowledge you if you're captured and we probably wouldn't be able to rescue you until our soldiers reach New Orleans," General Sharpe added.

Both Sarah and Cleota nodded in agreement.

"Ladies, would you step out of the room and let us discuss this a few moments?" the general replied.

Stewart rose and bowed to the two women. He closed the door as the ladies passed toward the rear of the central hallway.

"Truly, Miss Sarah Turner and Cleota do seem good candidates for this job," General Sharpe said.

Stewart rose and paced the floor. "Her tours with her father through the south give her a unique perspective on the river locations and the people. She has a creative mind, great intelligence and a practical education. She and Cleota speak French."

General Sharpe raised his arm, palm outward, "Out of character, she does have an aristocratic manner. Her servant appears equally qualified. I'm against this in principle, but I will agree, if you men think this will work."

The three others nodded..

General Sharpe continued, "If Miss Sarah and Cleota continue, we have over one hundred secret agents throughout the confederacy. These two should be able to connect with several we've placed in that area. Otherwise their identity would be kept secret and they must not be contacted directly by friends or family members while on assignment. This also might be difficult for one so young."

Stewart Bland commented, "Her father is recovering well from the wounds he received in the attempted robbery, I feel the separation will not prove a hindrance."

"They can pass censored notes to their family, but only through the channel of a contact agent. They can not reveal their location or assignment," General Sharpe cautioned.

The men bowed their heads, but each nodded his approval when General Sharpe called on them individually.

When Sarah and Cleota were called back into the room, General Sharpe revealed, "We've located the man who directed the robbery in which Daniel Roberts was killed, and your father and uncle wounded. We believe he directed his henchmen in the attempted robbery."

Sarah stiffened. Cleota reached for her hand.

The General noted their emotional reaction. "If you are too closely connected, or too emotional, you will be of no value to us," he warned.

"You must know that we are reluctant to appoint civilians as young as yourself, Miss Sarah." The older gentleman turned aside, "It is your decision."

"Will there be danger for Cleota, in a slave state?" Sarah asked.

"There could be."

Sarah turned toward her friend. Cleota nodded.

"We want you to know that you are not obligated. Personally I do not think you are the ones for this job," the general spoke gruffly.

Sarah rose with dignity, "Sirs, Cleota and I have discussed this assignment thoroughly. We are both in agreement to undertaking this task. We are committed to bringing this murderer to justice. We're abolitionists and we love our country."

"You cannot let your desire for revenge cloud your thoughts," one committee member said. "If you allow that to happen, you could reveal our whole plan. You and your contacts could all die."

"What makes you think you can carry this off?" General Sharpe asked.

"Tell me what you saw when you entered the house," Sarah spoke softly.

"Uhh— "

"You assumed we were southern women?" Sarah asked.

"Yes, I have to agree with you there," the committeeman answered.

Stewart interrupted, "Did I prove my point?"

"And that was?" General Sharpe asked.

"People don't notice servants."

"Or slaves, it appears," Cleota added.

"I plead guilty. I didn't look closely at you two ladies and could not have described you, had I been asked." The elderly committee member apologized. "I am sorry, I will attempt to do better next time."

"Do you know what you are letting yourselves in for?" another member asked.

"We are committed, regardless of the circumstances," Sarah stated. "We've both been in the south and they have flaws in thinking of southern women as objects without a brain in their heads. Slaves are overlooked as being fixtures that do not think or hear."

The three men conferred quietly.

The General rose to send the women on their mission.

"Upon my protest, but by the recommendation of your friend, Stewart Bland, we are going to appoint you. From now on, our operatives will train you. We will send you to Pinkerton's female operatives in Washington for interrogation training. This committee will have no further conferences with you. We don't wish to compromise this mission. If, before you reach New Orleans, you change your minds, let your contacts know of your decision."

"God speed, ladies. I admire your courage, but am concerned about all the rest."

Sarah patted the general's arm as he turned to leave, "We'll be fine. Don't worry about us."

"I'm afraid I do," he said softly.

The three officials left the parlor. They plucked their hats from the hall tree.

"I pray we aren't being foolhardy," General Sharpe muttered to his companions.

In the parlor, Stewart shook Miss Sarah and Cleota's hands. "You're on your way, hope I haven't made a grave mistake here."

The ladies spoke as one, "You haven't."

Stewart bowed and left the room.

Sarah turned to her friend, "Well, Cleota, I guess we're ready."

"Seems that way," Cleota agreed.

Agents of the Federal Government trained Sarah and Cleota. The officials suggested methods of operation and possible problems as they laid out many alternatives to the pair. The two specially trained female officers spent hours in their interrogation. At times agents who were strangers to the pair stepped into roles of military and civilian interrogators to further test the two.

Finally, Sarah and Cleota were as well-trained and prepared as humanly possible. Even exhausted and cruelly tested, they gave the *agreed upon* answers to the general descriptions of their situations. Other answers would require *always* playing their character roles: Sarah, a young orphan child from up country and her slave, Cleota.

One agent directed the pair, "Despite your grueling training, much of your safety will depend on your own native intelligence— your ingenuity and concentration. Use the encryption given to you by your contact for your messages. This will be changed often. Never allow these messages out of your control until passed to your contact. Take no chances on interception of any messages."

"It is imperative you follow the directions as you receive them in all your activities."

Final plans were laid before the two, "Montgomery Adkisson has made a contact. We expect him to lease our selected house within the next several months. He travels extensively in acquiring supplies and financing for the confederacy."

"We must get you into New Orleans and established in the selected residence before our suspect returns."

"Miss Sarah and Miss Cleota, we are placing you in this home. If all goes as we plan, we expect this old mansion to be used for Confederate activity."

"Sarah, your Turner name will be changed to Tourn'e. Cleota, you will be installed as a slave in the house. Keep your first names. Both of you will be required to play the parts. Your lives and this investigation will depend upon you."

"Total secrecy of your true identity will be required. Neither of you can slip up on names, that's why we elected to allow your first names to be used"

"We've learned that Montgomery Adkisson definitely ordered the seizure of your father's payroll, just as you suspected. He's been seen in and around New Orleans and we are expecting to complete our initial dealings with him very soon. Our contacts are attempting to entice him to our residence and chosen estate in the city," General Sharpe's aid explained again. "We hope that our plans for the estate and your interaction with Mr. Adkisson materialize."

"Are you ladies ready?"

Sarah sucked in a deep breath and nodded her head.

Cleota spoke for both, "Yes, 'bout as ready as we can be."

Citizens of New Orleans

In the peaceful New Orleans mansion, Sarah was no longer recognizable as the child of the owner of Turner Iron Works. She hadn't been south for some time or the months during her father's recovery. Only a few scattered merchants from Memphis toward the south could possibly recognize her. Certainly New Orleans was a land of merchants and exchange, but within a quiet household, and in disguise, she did not expect to encounter anyone who knew her or her father previously.

Middle American by birth, she slipped easily into speech that fit her purposes. After working with the household slaves a few months, only the most discriminating ear could pick up any speech pattern foreign to the south. If anyone had suspicion, her speech irregularities could be attributed to the eccentric speech of a backwater child.

Cleota fell easily back into the slave personae of her youth.

After they settled into their roles in the old mansion, the garden or Sarah's bedroom were the only truly private places where she and Cleota could openly converse. They used routine bedtime preparation for each day's assessment.

"Papa was up and down the Mississippi and adjoining rivers. Mama and I stayed in Missouri. Everyone doted on me until my mother died near my third birthday. After that, you and I went with Papa on his business trips on the river. As you remember, my education *was* unusual; I'm familiar with the towns and the people of the river. It was a game for me when I was able to blend into any place or people where we found ourselves. I amused myself by playing those imaginary parts during those long hours on the steamboat when Papa was involved in business transactions. Remember?

Sometimes Papa let me dress as a boy when he was into touchy dealings, so I could be with him and not distract from his work. Occasionally, we rode away from the Mississippi on horseback to complete his business or procure cotton to fill the steamboat on our return trips."

Sarah continued, "I was in many places, but I liked the Arcadian Valley in Missouri the best of the places we visited. It was unusual and so beautiful. Those folk were Unionists and most of them didn't keep slaves. Those were independent Yankees. I envied them their large related families and homey farms. They furnished charcoal for Papa and iron ore for the foundry."

" I've seen them all, good men and bad. This isn't too different. Papa said I was a shrewd judge of human nature. I learned that from him, I expect."

Cleota put in, "You inherited part of that and you're more like twice your age. Your papa was strict and you learned what's right at his side." A melancholy tone came to her voice, "You still live by his example."

"I don't like deceiving people. *That's* not what he taught me," Sarah said.

"You don't have any choice, child. Sometimes we have to do things we know aren't right to get somethin' that is right. We see that ever' day, all you gotta do is walk outside this house," Cleota added.

" I learned about being a lady, at your knee and across your lap." Sarah laughed, "I wasn't always happy about that."

"Your papa and mama freed me, but it wasn't always easy."

"After Mama died, you were my family and lived in my

room. I miss you being with me all the time here." Sarah placed her hand on Cleota's shoulder.

Cleota patted Sarah's hand. "We have to pretend. If I didn't stay in my own bed, or lay here on your floor, someone in this house would find our friendship unusual. We can't take that chance," Cleota commented.

"I hate your pretending to be a slave, it's demeaning. You can quit this anytime you need to."

"I'm fine. It's what I want to do. It'll be over one of these days. I can't quit, I'd never leave you in this God-forsaken man's presence alone!"

"We won't talk about this again, but you know what to do if you have to. You can go to Fuqua's store and get help," Sarah added.

಼

They took their task seriously and continued their *character* practice in the solitude of their outside garden chores. The two ladies named possible problems and together worked out plausible answers to every question they could imagine might arise. To eliminate the possibility of a discovery and loss of contact, they updated each other as to the latest happenings. Should one become unable to function in her chosen role, and to remain safe, each of them required duplicate stories and information.

಼

In the household, only Sarah and Cleota knew that the young master had been secretly led into the lease of the stately old mansion. The northern plan was perfectly set into motion.

The household fell into, seemingly, *normal routine* for the next months.

In New Orleans, Sarah had only three friends upon whom she knew she could always depend. Cleota, her friend and mentor; Gideon, the tiny crippled neighbor slave boy she befriended; and Clem, her Yankee contact at Fuqua's General Merchandise. No other federal contact was personally known by any of the three. If emergency arose, messages were to be sent by Sarah or Cleota, to Clem at the mercantile store. Her other help came from the innocent slave boy who carried nonstrategic messages to Clem. Important messages went to a crack in the mausoleum at the Ross Family Cemetery. Neither she, nor Cleota knew who retrieved or read their messages. They knew by experience that the message was always gone the next day when one of them casually took flowers to be placed at the grave, or knelt to pull weeds from the base of the marble edifice.

The bronze monument plate was for a woman, who discreetly served as Sarah's *ancient and silent confidant*, however they did not go oftener than necessary to the cemetery.

Any one with suspicions would have difficulty following three very *insignificant workers* going about their daily, mundane duties.

ᔑ⬩

In the following year, several incidental pieces of information were passed eithe rby cemetery notes, or to Clem at the store.

With the passage of time and minor successes, the ladies grew more complacent and discouraged in their quest for important strategic information.

With continued contact, Sarah's resolve softened toward Montgomery Adkisson. She frequently reminded herself, *I've good reason to dislike what he's done and continues to do.* She schooled herself on his misdeeds to keep her mind and the fires of revenge alive.

ᔑ⬩

In their second December, New Orleans' thermometers registered an unseasonably cold twenty-eight degrees, accompanied by a drizzly downpour.

Sarah lingered in the hallway, dusting the waxed furniture. She heard the chilled young master burst into his study where Cleota poked in the fireplace to restore a cheery blaze.

Accustomed to his moodiness and shows of temper with the household slaves, Cleota rose unsteadily and began to back from the room with the hot poker forgotten in her hand.

"Get me a whiskey, can't you see that I'm frozen?"

She moved to the sideboard, "Yes, Massa." Her hand shook as she poured from the crystal decanter. Several inches of whiskey splashed into the heavy glass. Cleota tapped the poker on the andiron and plunged it, sizzling into the half full glass.

The master whirled, "What are you doing?"

"Ole Massa like his whiskey hot when he cold." She held the glass as far as her outstretched hand would reach. He snatched it.

Cleota moved toward the door.

"Be gone!" Tipping back the glass, he gulped a mouthful, sputtered and spit. "What are you tryin' to do, scald me? Get out of my sight, or I'll use that poker on your face!"

She scrabbled from the room, fearful to relinquish the poker to the angry young man.

Sarah overheard from the hallway. She motioned Cleota toward the kitchen and entered the study.

"Can I help you with your toddy? The old master preferred his hot. He said it warmed his bones."

"That voodoo witch, tried to scald me!"

"Try a sip of water. Surely, the poker was hotter than she realized. Let me cool it down for you." She mollified the master, and splashed a few drams of whiskey into the warm glass. "I doubt she could tell how hot it was through this heavy glass. This seems about right."

He tipped it tentatively to his lips. "Yes— this is better."

"I'll speak with her. It won't happen again."

"See that you do," he spat.

When the young master rented the house, he was told that Sarah was fourteen and a half years old.

The estate's representative had worked well with their cover story, "She is an orphan that goes with the house. She has only an old uncle upcountry that lives in such a mosquito-ridden hole, it is unsafe for her to reside there for any length of time. For her livelihood, she will assist the slaves in the upkeep of this beautiful old place."

"She's rather young for such a responsible position?" he commented.

"Give her a try, if you're not satisfied, I'll find another place for her elsewhere."

In the eighteen months which followed, there had never been any reason to have Sarah relieved.

Montgomery Adkisson didn't know and didn't concern himself with the personal affairs of his household servants. That Sarah was a twenty-two year old Yankee would have greatly shocked him.

The neighbors grew to expect her presence. It seemed to them, she had always been there. As an undercover operative, she blended into the household's background.

The war advanced every day, giving the citizens of New Orleans more pressing concerns than the servants in their neighbor's household.

Most of the servants were acquired with the property. They remained in place; others were gradually introduced into the household, with Sarah endearing herself to them with her polite and kind manners. She became their director and co-worker.

At the neighboring estate, she had befriended a young crippled slave boy. Gideon's owner had thought him too weak to work, hence the boy was not missed and no requirements were made on his time. His master was glad to have the boy absent from sight. He had considered the child a poor bargain when he took the boy in with a work gang. The able-bodied slaves had been funneled to the sugar cane fields, but the boy was left to reside in the carriage house in the city.

Gideon remained out of sight and consciousness of those at Mr. Granger's town house. The boy's diminutive stature hid a keen intellect and loyal soul, easily influenced by kindness and concern from another. Sarah was the only human that showed him either.

Wrought iron fences separated the two beautiful and extensive properties, but did not screen occupants, or communication. Treats and conversation flowed through the fence at chance opportunities. Night or day, a bird tweet furtively called either the boy, or Sarah, to the fence.

In the household, Adkisson gradually entrusted Sarah to assist with his correspondence. Often she prepared his work when he was gone.

Each day, as directed, she cleared the master's desk, addressed the mail; and separated the incoming communications into little piles of bills or personal messages. She was instructed to lay aside those incoming messages with seals.

Montgomery Adkisson often called her into his study to personally write messages for him. She offered no comments in this service, but had a good hand and willingly cooperated in this additional duty. Both had ulterior motives in this cooperative venture; he, to direct messages in handwriting other than his own; she, to secretly gain intelligence information from her enemy.

At times, he asked her to add differing names on his correspondence. Her seeming lack of interest lulled the man into complacency in the messages he sent and made her appear less than intelligent to him.

ॐ

As spring advanced, the war crept closer and closer to New Orleans. Constant fear permeated the Crescent City's atmosphere as the effects of war controlled the household.

Alone, Montgomery Adkisson manipulated two messages on his desk. Careful consideration had gone into their composition. Purposely, the letters were written to *appear* as intelligence information on a new confederate troop movement.

A shout in the street diverted the attention of those within. Montgomery Adkisson hurried from the house. He carried his heavy gold-headed walking cane.

Sarah hurried to the desk to read the messages that had consumed so much of the young master's attention and countless pages thrown into the waste bin. The past three quarters of an hour had been occupied by feverish activity on his part. He had not summoned her and now she needed to know why.

These may be important. Hurry!

The first line on the page read, *Bring your group from the west into Canal Street.* The other made no sense to her. She recited the two messages over and over in her mind to memorize their content.

He did not return that day, or the next.

After reporting to her contact, Sarah fretted. *The messenger usually arrives at dusk each Tuesday evening, and the envelopes are still not addressed. I can wait no longer. I'll address the two messages according to his most recent directive, copy the addresses from the tops of the letters and seal the communiqués.* As she blew on the warm red wax, she heard the courier's three short raps on the rear door of the house.

As before, she took the two messages and others from the upper right-hand corner of the desk. She quietly went down the back hall, opened the door and handed out the messages. The messenger kept to the shadow of the house. This figure's cloak, the same dull gray as always, blended into the night. Sarah was unable to identify the small person.

Unknown to Sarah, her boss' intention had been to switch the messages. His intention was to give false information to the enemy in order to deceive them into a cleverly laid ambush. Plans had been made for the message's interception while going through Yankee-held territory and his hoped-for interpretations of the messages.

Montgomery Adkisson strolled into his office Wednesday morning with the sunlight streaming through the mullioned windows onto the center of his desk. He set his cane against the accustomed corner of the desk, hung his hat on the corner of the side chair and looked at his desk.

Cleared! Panic struck. He pulled the servant's bell chain sharply.

"Sarah, come here at once!"

She hurried in. "Yes, sir?"

"Where are my messages?"

"I addressed them as you've always directed and gave them to the messenger last evening." She carefully studied his face. His mouth opened and he blanched, then turned his back to her.

"Where did you send them?"

"To the names at the top, like always. They went out with the usual messenger last evening. I was afraid you wouldn't be back in time to send them and he arrived as I finished sealing the last one. He only comes once this week."

"Umh-"

"Was that right?"

"Yes— Yes, that's fine. That's all for now."

She left silently, but not before noting that he turned to pick up his cane.

Over the months, in routine house chores she had discovered the cane sheathed a sword within its length. Like many southern gentleman, he also carried a derringer up his sleeve. The small, but heavy gun, easily noted when the household staff brushed his outer garments.

She hurried quietly out the back door and to the huge drapery of leathery-leaves on the ancient magnolia tree at the edge of the property. A sweet bird sound echoed over the grounds. A black shadow slipped into the shade and listened. Neither figure could be seen from the master's study.

"Gideon, take a basket for vegetables from the back of our carriage house, follow the young master. If he looks back, act as if you're buying something. Here's a coin. Hurry, but don't let him see you. If he should notice you, slip away. Act dumb should he speak to you. See who he talks to, listen if you can. Be very careful, he's dangerous."

The brown clad shadow crept away unseen into the damp chill.

Adkisson walked briskly to the newspaper office and stuck his head into the door.

Gideon could not hear what was said, but the copy boy came out on the boardwalk. The two talked jerkily and then Adkisson turned on his heel. He looked both ways, across the street, then walked away quickly.

Gideon paid the grocer for greens and sauntered along in the shadows of the building, noting the copyboy left the side door of the printing office and walked in the same direction as the young master.

Adkisson stopped at a saloon and signaled to a dealer at the card table.

Gideon strolled past. Adkisson came from the saloon, again checked both directions and walked past the young slave who fingered meager spring produce next door. The boy lingered over the remaining shriveled vegetables. The card dealer came from the saloon, buttoning his coat hurriedly. A shadow followed the men down the street.

At a rooming house, the three men met in the hallway

and climbed the front stairs to a room on the third floor. After quietly knocking, they slipped inside.

Familiar with the city, Gideon slipped up the back stairs. Then listened through the rickety hallway stairs.

"The messages were sent to the wrong places, we must change our directions and do the opposite. I concocted the messages to give the impression of advance from the west, now we must get the message to our cooperatives for an advance from the east."

"That will work just as well. We'll have to hurry to get there ahead of their move!"

"That's fine, I'll send King out with a special message when I go by the livery stable. We know what we're doing, so that will be fine. No hitch in our plans this time."

"How did the mix-up happen?"

"It was a mistake. *A mistake, that won't happen again*!" Adkisson said.

A chair scraped and movement sounded from the room.

Gideon crept down the stairs. Before he reached the bottom of the steps, he heard voices. A door closed. The voices receded as the men went down the front stairs to the second floor.

Gideon waited behind the building until he saw each of the three pass across the alleyway from the front of the building.

Gideon hurried to the garden with his message for Sarah. He was able to relay what he had heard, nearly word for word. He gave descriptions and work details on each of the two men who met the young master.

Sarah walked back and forth, seemingly on an aimless stroll beneath the shadows of the magnolia. She fingered a leaf here and there. Finally, she made up her mind. She whispered softly as she sniffed a frost-wilted blossom.

"Gideon, go to the Fuqua store and tell Clem I need

two yards of mosquito netting delivered immediately!" With the cold, Sarah knew mosquitoes would be quiet for several weeks, but she needed to see Clem and prepare as soon as possible.

"Yes, Missy." Gideon faded from the shadows.

Sarah continued to walk in the quiet of the garden, she fingered the plants as she wandered the paths. Had anyone seen her, they would have assumed she was examining the remaining flowers for frost damage

❦

Fellow conspirator against the Federal government, Lawrence Asden called on Montgomery Adkisson in mid-afternoon. A grizzled butler showed him into the study and announced the big man's presence.

"Massa Asden. Suh."

"Come in, come in. Seat yourself."

The visitor waited until the butler disappeared down the darkened hallway.

"You may have to get out of this house before long. The Yanks are coming and they may be on to you."

Sarah came into the room quietly. "Is there anything you need for refreshments, Sir?"

"Do you wish refreshment, Lawrence?"

Asden turned his eyes to Sarah and gave her his full appraisal.

Adkisson spoke again, "Lawrence— do you want a drink?"

"No. No, not now."

"I'll ring if we need anything."

Sarah left as quietly as she had come, fading into the background.

"Who was that? I've never seen her here before."

"She's an orphan servant who went with the house."

"Do you have any, uh, interest toward her?" Asden asked speculatively.

"No."

"Are you sure? She's going to be a beauty some day."

"I hadn't noticed."

"Well, you might just take a look."

"No, she's not my type."

"Don't have to be your type for some things," Asden smirked. "If you catch my meaning?"

"She doesn't interest me in the least. She's just a little house mouse helping around here for her keep. She directs the slaves when I'm gone, writes letters for me when I don't want to have my handwriting recognized. She never asks any questions. I hardly know she's around."

"How old is she?"

"By now, I would guess about sixteen."

"Well, you do know something about her."

"I know she has an old uncle, upcountry in *mosquito hollow*, and she can't go there to live with him. Sometimes I'm not sure of her intelligence. She's harmless, that's about all I need to know!"

"If you say so? But I wouldn't bet on it."

Listening, outside the door, Sarah felt her face burn with embarrassment. *Be careful,* warned a voice inside her head. *I was recruited for this job, because I resembled a child. I've got to be sure I stay one as long as I'm needed here. These are evil men and they deserve to be caught. If I can help, I'm here to see this through.*

ૐ

The next day, in his office, the young master turned to Sarah. "Why do you go to the cemetery?"

She turned to look frankly into his face, innocence and vulnerability ever-present in her expression.

"Sometimes, when I miss my mother, I go to the cemetery to converse with a grand motherly woman I used to know."

"I looked at that tombstone, the date is very old. You

would have been very young when she died."

Sarah was quick to respond. "I suppose my memory of her is vague, but she seemed very loving to me— perhaps it's my imagination, but I *think* I can remember her."

"Perhaps, but it has to be more imagination than reality."

"I don't really know, but the cemetery is very peaceful with those old oaks draped in Spanish moss and the magnolia blossoms in the spring."

"I just wondered—" he looked away.

He seems embarrassed. Sarah looked away.

"Now about these letters." He lifted a small stack of completed messages and noted others, as he touched them with his index finger.

"Yes, Sir?"

"These need to go out today— You can wait until Thursday on this pile. I'll be leaving tomorrow for several days. Post these."

"Yes, Sir."

"That will be all for now."

She nodded her head and rose to leave the room.

The young master stared after her for a moment, then reached for his cane and hat.

Early the next morning, Sarah spoke to Cleota, "Come with me to the garden, the vegetable beds need weeding."

Cleota hurried to the pegs where their bonnets hung; gardening gloves inside the gathered crowns. She handed Sarah's to her and donned her own. The two leisurely moved toward the dewy leaves of the house garden's raised beds. Sarah lifted her skirt over the damp and knelt on a folded feed sack. Her face was turned from the house and Cleota pulled weeds with her bonnet hiding her face. The conversation continued without outward sign of communication between the two. Steeled reactions were suppressed by their severe discipline.

Sarah spoke first, "We need to be more vigilant, Adkisson has questioned me."

She sighed, "We could almost have a happy life here, if we could occasionally forget why we're in this household, but I see things that go on in the streets and homes of the citizens of New Orleans. I sometimes forget what could happen to us, if we make a mistake." She continued, "He asked about my visits to the cemetery. Perhaps I should limit those for a time."

"What'd he say?"

"He asked why I went?"

What'd you tell 'him?"

"Sometimes when I'm lonely, I go to converse with the old woman buried there."

"What'd he think a that?"

"He thought the old woman was too old for me to know."

Cleota stilled her response. "How'd you handle that?"

"I mentioned that I wasn't sure if it was memory, or my imagination, but the surroundings soothed me."

"Did he say anything else?"

"He seemed to accept my explanation and went back to the business of his messages— I think he believed me."

"I fear for you. Be careful." An involuntary shiver went up Cleota's back.

"I think we'd better change the posting place for our messages. I need to stay away from the cemetery for a time."

The pair was quiet for a few moments.

"I'll have to go once in a while, to keep up appearances of reminiscing," Sarah added.

"Yes'um that would be best. You want me to take the next message?"

Sarah thought aloud, "We can't use Clem, we must save him for emergencies. I don't know, we'll have to see what develops."

Honey bees buzzed around their heads and mosquitoes hummed in the rich foliage.

Cleota raised her voice, "I think this bed's about clean. My knees are gettin' too stiff for this kind of work."

Sarah reached for the older woman's hand and assisted her to her feet. Cleota shook out her dress and bent to put the weeds on the feed sack where Sarah had knelt. She lifted the whole and dumped the small greens onto the refuse pile in the corner of the yard. She shook out the sack and folded it over her arm.

Sarah swept back a strand of dark hair from her forehead.

"Well, that's another bed. It's getting too hot for this kind of work, we'll finish tomorrow." *We must have mistress to slave appearance.* She spoke louder, "Pick up the sack and we'll go inside." She turned her back and wandered toward the kitchen door, snapped a blown flower or random dead leaf from the flowering plants in her seemingly, aimless progress along the path.

Cleota, accustomed to her role, did as Sarah had instructed, then turned casually to look over the gardens, at the windows of the big house, and beyond the fence. *No one in sight, but can't let down.*

A merry twitter sounded from beyond the wrought iron fence, and was acknowledged by Sarah waving away a mosquito from her damp face. *Nothing going on today, no need to respond to that particular question from Gideon.*

Federal Intelligence Headquarters

Stewart Bland and General Sharpe's recently returned aide conferred.

"You knew the retrieval site for S's messages has changed?" the young man confided.

"Yes. Why was that?" Stewart asked.

"It was at her initiative, she must have suspected that someone was becoming suspicious. In this kind of work, it's always good to prevent locking into a consistent pattern."

"Yes, you're right. She's creative and I'm sure she had a good reason." Stewart rubbed his chin. "We'll carry on, but get her word that we approve of her decisions. Warn her to take extreme care."

"We can't reveal all Adkisson's correspondence or he may become suspicious," the aide stated.

"In the position she's in, she's too valuable to waste. Let's disregard this information and examine future messages in light of the patterns we see developing," Stewart replied.

"I think that would be best. It's too dangerous to risk her this late in the game."

"See that she's informed. Continue to retrieve her messages, but ask her to send only crucial messages for a time until any suspicions may be diverted," Stewart directed.

❦

For appearance's sake, *pretend* slave and mistress innocently prepared for bed. Sarah sat in the center of her four-poster bed, Cleota on the top step of the ladder. They conversed quietly.

"Cleota, I'm very sorry I have been so bossy, but I have to act the housekeeper and overseer when we're in public. Forgive me?"

Cleota hugged Sarah. "Nothing to forgive. I understand fully."

Having learned to fade into the household and not draw attention to themselves, they worked constantly at their disguise. Sarah seldom left the house where she worked and had not been overly noticeable to Adkisson's business callers, who assumed her a paid housemaid. Cleota continued to play the perfect house slave, relying on her training before she came to Sarah's family and received her freedom.

Only one clandestine layer of the southern world came to their door through the dealings of the young master.

In Adkisson's absence, the household was at its most relaxed.

One morning, Lawrence Asden appeared on the doorstep already in his cups. With Samson outside working in the carriage house, Sarah opened the door for him.

"Missy, what's your name?"

"Sir, I'm Sarah." She stepped back from the door, attempted to push the door closed. Asden put his shoulder against the upper panel. Sarah tried for a courteous distance and formality.

He shoved the door open and lunged for her. Sarah stumbled, he wrapped his arm around her waist, drew her up to his rotund body, tried for her mouth, then smeared a kiss across her cheek before she could resist. She jerked away and he staggered, but he had his arms so firmly locked about her that he fell, pulling her down with him. His cane bounced away on the cool stone floor.

Sarah landed on top, but he rolled with her. She was pinned beneath him.

With the surprise and her small stature, she was overwhelmed by his weight. She kicked up with her knee, but failed to deter him.

He buried his face in her neck and strained against her.

She managed to let out a screech.

Suddenly, he lost his grip on Sarah, and was rolled aside.

She sat up and gasped for breath.

"What, what the— ?" Asden barked.

Cleota hammered the man with her fists. She released her pent-up frustrations from the last months upon him. He covered his head with his arms and roared.

Samson pulled Cleota from atop the man and pushed her into the dining room. She attempted to get by him.

"No. Youse stay there!" Samson growled.

The frightened butler turned to the huffing visitor, "Massa Asden, let me help youse up. Are youse hurt?"

Sarah rose to her feet and pushed by the pair. She opened the door to the dining room, went in, shut the door and hurried to Cleota.

She hissed, "Come with me. We've got to get you away from that man. No telling what he may do. Don't forget what you are supposed to be."

"Get me away! He oughtta be horsewhipped for what he tried to do to you."

"I know, but don't forget why we're here. Come on."

Sarah propelled Cleota out the servant's entrance in the dining room; through the kitchen; and out the back door. They hurried along the path to the carriage house and into the tack room.

"You've got to settle down. Stay here and I'll see what I can do. Don't go anywhere. Don't show your face in, or outside the house until he's gone. I'll come back for you as soon as I can."

Cleota buried her face in her arms. "I'm sorry, I forgot. That old man ought to be shot, but I forgot what I was supposed to do. Are you all right?"

Sarah held Cleota, "Thank you, you saved me. I'm fine. I'll be back as soon as I can." Sarah released Cleota, patted her and closed the door firmly behind her. *No one else knows where Cleota is hidden and I aim to keep it that way until this situation is calmed.*

As she passed the study, she overheard Asden's blubbering. She halted at the door. Adkisson had returned and was plying him with more whiskey. Samson stood with his head bowed.

"That old wench hit me with her fists!" Asden stormed.

Sarah had to strain to hear Adkisson's reply.

"Why did she do that?"

"No reason, it's the nature of the beasts, you should know that," Asden blustered. "They're uncivilized. Barely tamed. Can't trust them behind your back."

"Samson, do you know anything about this?"

"No, Suh. I pulled her off'em," Samson answered with his head bowed.

"Was there anyone else there?"

"Yes, Suh."

"Speak up man, who else was there?"

"Miss Sarah."

"Who— what did you say?"

"Miss Sarah, Suh."

Sarah stepped into the door opening.

Asden started to interrupt, disgruntled with Montgomery Adkisson's receiving information from any but himself. As he opened his mouth, his eyes locked with Sarah's. He closed his mouth without speaking. He rose unsteadily.

"Call for my carriage, I need to go home. Whip that slave and let's forget this matter."

Sarah started to protest, then thought better of it. *Better to keep quiet and let the matter drop, if that is possible.*

She retreated to her room, brushed up her hair and rinsed her face with cool water. She took several deep breaths and looked at herself in the mirror. She could not meet her own eyes. *Why do I feel so dirty? I didn't do anything wrong.* She soaped her hands again and heard the rumble of a carriage as it pulled away from the front walk. *I've got to take care of Cleota.*

When she passed quietly down the stairs, Montgomery Adkisson looked out. "Sarah come into the study."

She steeled herself for the encounter.

"That slave must be punished. I will not put up with her in my household any longer, sell her."

"Please don't. She was only protecting me. Surely you can understand that she feels loyalty to me. She's known me for a long time and cared for me when I was a child." Sarah's mind sought a quick answer, "If ever she failed, or when she got too old, I was to return her to my uncle."

"Protect you, what do you mean?"

"Oh, I'm sorry," Sarah looked down, embarrassed.

"What did you mean?" Adkisson asked.

Sarah was reluctant to speak.

A perfect example of the southern gentleman, gently the young master questioned, "You can tell me— Sarah." He spoke her name for the first time. "Go ahead," he urged.

I'm caught, I must say something. She sighed and kept her eyes averted. "Mr. Asden made unseemly advances, Cleota helped me."

"That's not hard to believe." He turned from her. "All right, you do something with her, but get her out of my sight, I never want to see her again." He turned toward Sarah and raised his hand for emphasis, "Make very certain that Asden doesn't see her anywhere near here, ever!"

"I'll see to it, first thing in the morning."

"Let's hear no more of it."

Sarah walked away with more thoughts of the strange customs of the south. *Politeness to whites, cruelty to Negroes. It's a strange mix of gentleness and dictatorship. I don't understand. Thank you, Lord for making it this easy for Cleota to be safe.*

ک

Sarah and Cleota waited until night for their discussion.

"Cleota, because of what's happened, you must go away."

"Missy, I can't leave you now," Cleota's voice caught.

Sarah was intense, "I can't protect you. He could even drag you bodily to the slave market, or have you beaten. He could even kill you. He told me to get you out of this household and out of his sight. If we don't get you out of here, all could be lost."

"No, miss."

"Be tough, Cleota, this is a necessity."

"I can't leave you at the mercy of— his *friends*. No one knows what they might do to you."

"I carry a derringer in my clothes at all times. We'll have to risk that I can take care of myself, otherwise our cause will be lost. We can't have that happen. I have a perfect situation here. We're beginning to get real information. Gideon lives close. He knows that if he hears a scream from this house, he is to go immediately to Clem at the store."

"If something happens at night, does Gideon know where Clem lives? " Cleota asked.

"Yes, he knows. It's been worked out with the two."

"I can't leave you after all these years. You're my baby!" Cleota clung to Sarah.

"But you must. There is no other way. Perhaps we can find a place for you to stay that is only a short distance. You must not show your face where the young master or Asden could see you."

"Yes," Cleota breathed.

Sarah thought for a moment, her attention diverted by the need for a strategy.

Cleota answered for her, "If a slave handler comes for me, we must put on a good show or the young master might get suspicious."

"We can't call too much attention, or it might work against us."

Sarah patted Cleota's hand. "I'll have Gideon take the message. We'll see what our connections think is best."

"Yes, missy." Cleota wiped a single tear from her eye; neither woman gave in to outward emotional displays. "Keep your head."

"You too. I'll get on with it." Sarah went to write the message for Gideon, then dropped the message by the fence when she emptied the ashes on the edge of the garden path.

Ten minutes later, no movement was seen, but a small brown hand reached for the piece of paper. Forty minutes later, the small cripple walked aimlessly down the center of the street as he wandered to the general store.

Sarah made a display of writing a letter to her uncle upcountry. She carried it to post that afternoon and dropped the undeliverable envelope into the mail slot.

ï▲·

A day later, Montgomery Adkisson stormed into his office. He startled Sarah as she dusted the books on the shelf.

"What about that slave?"

"I've made arrangements. She'll remain in the kitchen or in the quarters until the overseer comes. He'll be here as soon as he can from my Uncle's plantation. He'll take her."

A stab of compassion smote the young master. "Do you wish to accompany her to your old home?"

She studied his face. *What would be a southern attitude toward a slave?* Sarah raised her chin and spoke quietly, "No, that won't be necessary."

"Fine," he turned aside and busied himself with the papers on his desk. "I prefer you stay here to take care of my correspondence. See that I'm not involved in this transaction any further."

"Yes, Sir. I'll have her taken while you're away, probably on Saturday."

"See that you do. Now let's get on with our work," he ordered.

Sarah sat with a heavy heart for his dictation of another correspondence, one she did not understand but that carried many numbers. Her brain attempted to work along with her hand. *What do these numbers mean? Coded. I can't possibly remember all these numbers.*

Panic seized her heart and mind. Doubling her agitation was her inability to understand the meaning of anything he told her to write.

"You seem distracted, do you want to stop?"

"Just for a moment. I'll be right back." Sarah rose and hurried from the room.

Montgomery stepped to the window and looked out over the street. Lawrence Asden alighted from his carriage and turned to look toward the house.

"I'll meet him outside. Hope he's in better shape, and humor, than last time." He picked up his cane, adjusted his hat, and went out the front door.

Sarah heard him leave and hurried into the office. She looked out the window to see him going up the front path. She faced the window to observe outside activity. Quickly, she copied the numbers on a scrap of paper and shoved it into her hidden skirt pocket with her derringer. The pistol's reassuring weight thumped against her flank when she smoothed her apron over her skirt. She left the foolscap page exactly as he'd left it and hurried from the room.

I can't understand this. I'll pass it along as is. If it's anything important, I hope and pray someone up the line can make sense of these numbers and statements.

Sarah left the house and wandered over the garden. Casualness and a troubled mind were the aim of her appearance. Acting the part was not hard to reproduce, she felt it.

Squatting to pick flowers, she placed several in her drawn up apron. In one of her snatches, she left the note amongst the leaves. With her face toward the ground, she gave a light bird tweet, then wandered away to other stalks of flowers. Out of the corner of her eye, she caught the brown hand as it reached for the note. She heard an answering tweet and rose to step to the next flowering plant. Her body covered the furtive movement from view of those within the house.

Other blossoms drew her attention. She neared the potting shed and reached for the clippers. She sheared the stems from her recently picked bouquet, piled the clipped blooms back into her apron, and moved toward the back door. She drew water from the cistern and plunged the stems into the water bucket, stretched, surveyed the gardens, then turned to go inside with her bouquet.

In a few minutes, Gideon delivered the encoded message to Clem.

The next day, Sarah, lost in thought, walked toward Fuqua's. She was startled by a shout behind her.

"Stop that slave. He stole my money."

A man brushed her rudely aside as he passed and grabbed an old man walking in front of Sarah.

"I've got him!"

The young ruffian threw the old man roughly to the street.

A passerby stepped down from his buggy with his

whip in his hand.

"Give him a good one. Here, use my buggy whip."

Sarah drew back, *No trial, no other information.*

The two men began beating the old man. He lay on the ground with only his head covered by his arms. As a final blow, the owner of the whip gave him a kick in the side.

A parish policeman arrived, as the old man groaned and doubled to his injured side. The old Negro was lifted from the ground by the constable and pushed toward the slave jail. The crowd turned aside, their entertainment for the day ended.

Sarah reached for the constable's arm "Stop! Can't you stop treating him so roughly? Can't you see, he can barely walk? Help him, please." Tears rolled down Sarah's face. The lawman looked at her in confusion, but put his shoulder under the old man's arm and assisted him on his way. Another man sneered at her. She turned away.

Oh, Lord, help that man. I can not do this. I can't stand to see him mistreated, but I have to look toward the others involved. Please, Lord, make it easier for him. Help me know what to do.

She turned for one last look at the old man being helped down the street and headed for home, too upset to stay in public or run her errand.

By her bed that night, she prayed. *Lord, I'm so angry. Does my anger help anyone? Please help me keep a clear head and know what I'm supposed to do. I'm not Solomon, I don't have his wisdom. I can't win. If I help these people now, I won't be helping them in the future.*

I can't draw attention to myself, like I did today. But I did help that old man, a little. Dear Lord, help him recover from the treatment he got today. Help him be healed. Let him know that someone cares.

Please let those men think that I was just a girl who didn't want to see cruelty. Don't let them be suspicious of my actions and cause my friends any trouble. Don't let this get back to Mr. Adkisson, or if it does, let him not think anything is unusual. Please let me know what I'm to do and— please give me some peace about it. Thank you, Amen.

ᘒ⬧

Thursday when she went into the store, Clem sidled toward her. "I have someone you must meet."

"When and where?"

"Here. Come Tuesday morning at ten."

"I'll be here then." She continued, "Were the numbers of value?"

"I couldn't add them, but maybe others could. We don't have to know," Clem said.

"You're right." *Am I doing any good with all this- whatever it is?*

"How is she?" she asked discreetly of Cleota.

"Fine, out of sight, but nearby," Clem replied.

That night, Sarah offered special prayer for her new dilemma.

Dear Lord, help me succeed in this mission and the new developments. There's always a risk when we have new contacts. I'm sure others are careful, but Lord, help me to say and do the right thing. I've already gotten Cleota into trouble; please don't let anyone else get hurt. Keep Cleota safe. I miss her. Keep me safe to complete my work here.

There is no one I can talk to about what I'm doing, no one with whom I can ever let down my guard.

Let this war be over soon so Cleota and I can go home and see Papa. Please keep him well. Protect us all. I haven't heard from him for so long. Maybe I can send a message to him indirectly. I need to know how he is and that someone out there still loves me.

Be with Gideon, heal his body and make him strong, keep him from being punished for what he can't do. Protect him from servitude. He's such a grand little man. Thank you for him. Thank you for making him my friend.

Thank you for Clem and this new contact, whoever he may be. Keep us all in your will and allow us to do our job well. Please help us get this over, soon! Thy will be done. Amen.

On Tuesday, Sarah looked around when she entered the store. Clem was alone. He looked up, then inclined his head toward the bolts of cloth in the rear.

"Hello, Miss Sarah."

A strange young man's head appeared above the table. Under black brows, electric-blue eyes consumed Sarah. She was shocked by the intensity of the stare and felt inspected to her very soul. Her gaze shifted to the balance of the face and she saw the quirk of a smile start at one corner of his full lips.

Clem slipped along the counter so that their conversation would not be interrupted, should other customers enter the store.

"This is Samuel Henri. He's to take C's place. He lives on the Henri shrimper out of the Gulf."

Sarah spoke to Samuel for the first time. "Hello."

"Same to you."

"How am I to contact you?"

"Same as before."

Footsteps were heard at the front of the store. Samuel sank below the shelf as a rustle entered. He faded out the storeroom door, unseen by those entering.

Sarah fingered the fabric and sighed. *Not a personal replacement for Cleota, just another contact. Lord, I'm getting lonely in this job. Help me persist and be patient.*

Sarah lingered until the lady left with her precious bag of corn meal.

"Well, what did you think?"

"Couldn't tell. Too short a time."

"He's all right. I've known him for almost two years."

"You said he lived on a shrimper?"

"Yes, he's lived with them long enough that most people think he's a Cajun. He even goes by their last name. He's good with their language."

"I didn't notice a Cajun accent," she replied.

"With others he'd have it, but he knows who and what you are. It wasn't necessary for him to use it. He thought you might not understand him."

"Kind of scruffy looking."

"That serves his purposes. He looks, acts, and speaks the part. That's all most need to see."

"Yes. I guess I'm one to talk," Sarah sighed and looked down at her worn apron.

"He'll be here again next Thursday about nine in the morning. You can get better acquainted then. We'll vary the time. If anyone chances to see you together, they won't notice, he's a lady's man. Folks will think he's found someone else to flirt with."

Sarah turned shocked eyes to Clem, "He's a lady's man?"

"Don't be shocked, lots of fellows can't help it. Like a magnet, we collect those iron fillings."

"You considering yourself one too?" she asked.

"Can't you tell?" Clem grinned.

Sarah laughed, one of the few she'd had lately.

"Ease up Sarah. Life does go on, you do understand?"

"Hard to imagine at times like these." She turned to go.

"I'll be seeing you whenever you need something."

"Yes, good-by-   and thanks," she dropped her hand to the handle of her produce basket.

"That's okay, and don't forget- anytime," Clem said.

That night as Sarah drifted into sleep, she was haunted

by the intensity of those blue eyes.

I guess he has to look carefully at his contacts. That's the only way we can stay alive and useful. I shouldn't let it bother me- but it did. It does. I can't let this- the way I feel interfere with my work. I was put here and the bosses select who I should work with. That's the way it is and I'll have to accept him, even though I feel strange about him.

The next Thursday, she nonchalantly walked to the store with a basket over her arm. As before, she saw no one when she entered the front door. She browsed toward the rear and faced the back wall of goods.

"Keep doing what you're doing. I'm here."

Sarah's head jerked around. "How is C? Have you seen her?"

"She sent you her love, but she worries about you."

"So far, so good. Tell her that I love her."

"I'll not see you again until Clem tells you, or you need to make contact."

A customer entered the store. Clem cleared his throat.

Sarah moved from the meager bolts of cloth to the cracker barrel.

"Add a half dozen of these to my list."

Later when she looked for her contact, he was gone.

That night, Sarah's loneliness for Cleota got the better of her. She retired to be alone with her melancholy.

The house grew quiet. Sarah drifted toward sleep. A pair of intense eyes dogged her memory.

She was jolted awake by the sound of pounding on the front door.

Samson, ever on duty, plodded to answer the door.

Wrapping her hooded cloak about herself, she slipped into the hallway outside her door, then part way down the stairs where she stopped in the shadows..

"Out of the way, ole man. I need to see your master!"

"He ain't here, Suh."

"Where is he?"

"I don't know, Suh."

Sarah stepped down with defiant chin, "I'm his house-keeper and secretary, may I help you?"

Startled, the embarrassed man turned toward her, cleared his throat and stared into the stairway gloom.

"Do you know when Montgomery will be back? I haven't got time to wait!"

"We're expecting him in the morning," Sarah answered in a cool manner.

"I've got a message for him. It's sealed and ready. Deliver it as soon as he comes in tomorrow, and *only to him*?"

"Certainly. I'll see that he receives it as soon as he arrives."

"No one else is to see this, do you understand?" Asden threatened, "It would go very hard if my orders are disobeyed!"

"I understand. You know that I handle much of Mr. Adkisson's correspondence. I'll take care of it. I've never failed him." Sarah tried to dismiss Asden's concerns.

"I have to leave town and he must get this message!"

She could see that he was agitated and had no alternative.

"Yes, I understand." Sarah received the message from his reluctant fingers.

"I'll be on my way then. See that you do as you're told."

Sarah hoping to hurry him out, stepped toward the door, "Good night, Sir."

Asden put his hat on as he rushed through the door.

Sarah shut the door quietly and checked the lock. The old butler faded back toward his bedroom.

She hurried to the top of the stairs and peered out the second story window. Asden's carriage careened around the corner. *He truly is gone.*

She tiptoed to each upper-story window and looked out into the night. No one stirred. Then she saw a shadow in the neighboring yard. *Gideon must have heard the noise and is up.*

Should I risk opening this message? She fingered the wax seal, drew the curtains and lighted a covered candle. She examined the seal, an "A" imbedded in blue wax. *We don't have any blue wax in the house. Should I risk Gideon's involvement? Yes, I think I must. I can't walk the streets at night, but he'll be almost invisible. This must be important if Asden's leaving the city and wanted the master to see it immediately.*

In her concealing black cape, she slipped downstairs and out the back door, tweeted the night bird sound and moved under the magnolia's dripping, leafy shroud. Gideon was there in the shadows to meet her.

"I don't know what is in this sealed message, but get it to C.D. tonight. Tell him that I *must* have it back by daylight. I'm to give it to Mr. Adkisson as soon as he returns. I was threatened. We'll all be in danger, if it is not returned. It must appear to be unopened and be returned in the same condition it is now."

She took the young boy's arms in her hands and looked into his face. "This is the most important thing I've ever asked you to do, Gideon. Tell him to be sure the same seal is used." Sarah turned the young boy and patted his back, "I'm sorry to send you out tonight, but I don't know what else to do." Sarah gave the boy a push toward the garden gate, "Can you do it?"

"Yes'um," Gideon answered.

"I'll be praying the whole time. Hurry, but don't get caught."

"I'se goin'."

"Thank you. Gideon, I love you."

"Me too, Ma'am." And he was gone.

Sarah stood under the tree shroud and looked for stars. There were none. A moldy scent rose from the damp earth. *At least it's dark, no one will be out in the middle of the night and no one will look for Gideon. Dear Lord, take care of him, as you did your Gideon in the Bible. Make his one little soul invisible to the enemy and ple-ese keep him safe! Let him hurry.*

She retreated toward her room, quietly listening to the noises of the sleeping house as she returned through the slave quarters and back up the stairs. As she passed the butler's rooms, she heard quiet murmuring. Unashamed of her surveillance, she listened. Josie and Samson discussed the rude awakening of the night, but all seemed well. She heard the rustling of their straw mattress as they settled back into night rhythm. In no time, she heard Samson's slight snoring as he returned to a peaceful sleep.

Sarah spent a restless night. She listened for the grandfather clock at the foot of the stairs.

"Bong, bong, bong, bong!" *Four in the morning, I can't stay in bed any longer.* She walked the floor. *Where is Gideon? Oh, Lord, did I send that child to his death? Please take care of him. Please help Clem know what to do and get it done quickly. Help me know what to say, if they don't finish with the message. I don't care about myself, but help me protect the others. Give me strength to do right by them.* She plucked at the bed coverings, the curtains—

At five, she dressed and went downstairs. She dusted and worked in the house until five thirty, then stepped out into the garden amongst the shadows. The dew was heavy on the lawns and a mist hung over the grounds. She crept to the enveloping shadows of the magnolia and began to whisper another prayer.

Her prayer grew so fervent, that she whispered aloud,

"Oh, Lord, protect my friends. Help the one get home safely. Please let him be all right."

"I'se here, Miss."

A sob escaped her throat. She knelt and clasped Gideon's hand to herself through the bars of the fence. "Are you all right?"

"Yes, and I got the job done." He opened his shirt and withdrew a starkly white envelope.

Sarah quickly placed the envelope safely into the pocket of her apron.

"Did C.D. get everything he needed done?"

"Yes, they opened the letter and they says it was 'portant. They copied, den put it back in a new envelope, 'xactly like the one it came out of. They copied the writin' on the outside and waxed it up just like it was before."

"Oh, thank you Gideon. I'm so sorry that I sent you. I shouldn't have."

"That's fine, Miss Sarah, I's glad to help. I slipped in the mud. That's why they had ta use a new envelope. I put the new'n inside my shirt so's it wouldn't happen on the way back."

"Did you hurt yourself when you fell?" she asked.

"No Ma'am. Jus' got a little more mud, dat's all."

"I'm so glad you're fine. Thank you again. I guess we'd better go in before someone sees us." Sarah touched her lips to his hand, rose and stepped back.

She slipped in the back door and heard stirring coming from the slave quarters. She hurried up to her room and took the envelope from her pocket. By the tiny light of her candle, she examined the envelope.

The writing looks exactly as it did before. The envelope looks good. She turned it over. The wax and the initial are fine. Oh, thank you Lord.

She collapsed on the side of her bed. A sob escaped from deep in her throat. She took several deep breaths.

Steadied herself and put the envelope back into her apron pocket.

If this message is so important, Mr. Adkisson would expect me to guard it with my life. I'll keep it in my pocket until I hear him come, then I'll take it to him myself. I won't risk any other hands. If something goes wrong, he will blame only me. Thank you Lord. Please help me finish this thing— and be calm when I see him.

After breakfast, Sarah entered the library and began straightening books and putting things in order. She fidgeted and steadied her nerves.

The young master strolled from the rear of the house, "Samson said you had something for me?"

"Yes, it's right here. I kept it in my apron pocket to be sure you got it first thing. Mr. Asden said it was very important and I didn't want to take any risks with it."

He reached for the envelope, looked at it and turned it to break the seal. Sarah tensed and turned away. She heard the rustle of papers as he extracted the pages from the envelope, then his indrawn breath as he digested the message. She turned back to observe his actions.

Agitated, he ran his hand through his hair, then seemed to recall that he was not alone.

"I won't need you for a time. Please go see to my breakfast, I didn't have time for that earlier."

Sarah moved from the room, mulled over the morning to herself. *He was kinder than usual, that was different. Everything seemed to go well. No suspicions. Thank you Lord! I think we made it this time.*

Potatoes?

When Sarah went to the next contact meeting at the store, Clem spoke, "Miss Sarah, we finally got a few potatoes in the backroom. You can go on back and pick what you want."

Sarah knew why she was directed to the back room. Her heart gave a jerk as she stepped to the darkened area.

A quiet voice sounded, "I'm here. Step in a little further and turn to your right."

Sarah obeyed. The light was dim. She could make out very little of the form before her.

Clem stepped back out of the room. "Just bring your potatoes out front when you decide what you want." No one was in the store, but he kept up the pretense to avoid suspicion should anyone overhear.

Sarah whispered a quick thought, "I must remember to bring out potatoes when I leave the storeroom."

"I don't have any information for you today, but I thought we'd better get acquainted before anything comes up. As far as you know, I'm a shrimper and I live on the Henri boat. We go out for days at a time, but Clem knows how to reach me. In the capacity I serve, I'm in and out of port. Through the selling of our shrimp, I come into contact with *many* people."

"I understand. Have you heard from C?"

"Yes, I'm directed to tell you that she is fine and living

on Canal Street."

"She is here in the city?" Sarah asked.

"Yes," he said.

" I'm glad, in a way. Are you sure she's safe there?"

"Yes, it was decided that she might need to be an operative again and it was best that she stay in the city for now. She's in seclusion and no one sees her."

"I'd like to see her, or at least, send her a message."

"I'll see what can be arranged, but I wouldn't bank on it. It's risky that someone might see the two of you. As far as *they* know, she's in the back country."

"Yes, I'm sorry. I forgot and let down for a moment. Please tell her that I really miss her and am praying for her."

"She prays for you too. Better get your potatoes and go back out. Don't want you to take too long back here."

"Do you know where they are? The potatoes, I mean," Sarah asked.

"I'm sitting in the potato bin, I've already picked you out half a dozen."

"Thank you." Sarah saw the flash of very white teeth as warm fingers closed her hand over a large potato. She placed it in her basket and felt his hand touch her arm, as he held out another.

She spoke quietly, "No wonder you look a little scruffy, hanging about in potato bins."

"And on a shrimp boat."

"I didn't want to mention that, but I can tell where you are, without seeing you."

"I can even tell *where I am*. I've gotten used to it the last two years, but it wasn't pleasant at first. I don't eat shrimp anymore."

"I can imagine."

"I'll see you again soon. Clem will set a time, or you can let him know if you need anything."

"Thank you."

"*Thank you*, Miss Sarah," Samuel said.

When Sarah turned from the dim room, the light in the store briefly blinded her. She stumbled and would have fallen, had not Clem caught her upper arms. He steadied her, looked into her eyes, then quickly away.

He spoke to cover his confusion, "Here, here. It's dark back there, it's hard to see when you first come out. Are you all right?"

"Yes, but don't scare me like that. I didn't know who you were for a moment. I was afraid someone might have heard us."

"I stayed in the back of the store to make sure no one else did," he added.

"It seems as if all I do today is thank someone."

"That's a good thing to be doin'. We can't get enough help and can't be too grateful."

"Yes, well I best be going. Let me pay you for these potatoes."

"Come right up here and set them on the counter."

After Sarah paid for the produce, she turned to go. "Thank you."

They both laughed, sharing a joke.

"There you go again."

༄

Alone, lonely without Cleota, Sarah finally returned to the cemetery to voice her thoughts to the grave of her *old* friend. As she rounded an ancient live oak, a voice spoke to her from above. Drawn back suddenly from her reverie, she started. Her hand flew to her throat.

"It's Samuel," the disembodied voice spoke from the branches.

Sarah glanced around in all directions. "Are you sure it's safe here?"

"Yes, I checked it out before I came out and climbed up here. I followed you from the house until I figured you were coming here. Sit down at the base of my tree and we can talk."

Sarah spread her skirt and reclined casually against the tree.

"You know you are a lovely girl?"

Taken back, she hardly knew how to reply. "Clem told me you were a lady's man."

"He did not!"

"Yes, he did."

"Well, I'm not. That's just Clem's idea. Anyway, I've a few things to tell you and I'd better get to those."

"Proceed."

"Cleota sends her love."

"Thank you. Return mine to her, will you?"

"There is a shipment coming in on Friday. They plan to storm the port and try to take the city."

"Should you be telling me this?"

"Yes, they want you to keep an eye open. Determine if Adkisson or any of his cohorts have an inkling."

"He hasn't been as active with his messages lately, *or* I haven't been included."

"Are messengers coming more often?"

"No, and some weeks they don't come at all."

"We'll have to check that out. Send a message by your little friend or come to the store if you hear anything. I'll make a point of getting back to you if I learn anything that might help you. If a messenger comes, let C.D. know. If Adkisson gets information, we may need to waylay his reply."

"Is there anything else I need to know?"

"No, but stay here a little. I want to talk to you."

"Why?"

"Like you, there aren't too many I can normally talk to. I need to hear *Yankee* once in a while."

She picked up on his mood. "How did you learn to speak Cajun?"

"At first, I couldn't understand what they were saying at all, but I lived with the Henri's for awhile, before I knew their dialect came out."

"I know. I can speak French, but their version is very different."

"You speak French? How did you learn that?"

"Papa thought I should be well educated. He saw to it that I had a French tutor for a while. It helps to pick out a few of their Cajun words, but not much. Cleota learned more than I."

"She seems very intelligent."

"She's brilliant."

They were silent for a minute.

"I imagine you are too," Samuel added.

Sarah played with a long strand of grass. "What did you do before this war?"

"I was mercenary. I did whatever I needed to live. I came down here and met the Henri's. They fed me, had such a happy family, I just fell in with them and now I feel like one of theirs, but I can't tell them everything."

"Do you ever feel guilty?" Sarah asked.

"About what?" Samuel said.

"That you are deceiving the Henri family?"

"Yes, but they are an independent lot. They aren't for slavery. Some of the family have slave ancestry and are sympathetic to those in servitude. I convince myself that they would understand, *if* I could tell them about what I'm doing."

"Will you, someday?" she asked.

"Yes, I think I will."

"I'll never be able to tell Mr. Adkisson. He was responsible for my father's injuries and I haven't forgiven him for that." She held back personal information. "I'd like to confront him someday, but I don't know if that will ever happen. I have to be very careful not to let myself hate him. I don't think I could do my job if I think about him too much."

"I expect you're right," he agreed.

Sarah mused on, "My little friend knows some things, but I don't want to overburden a child. He and I are really friends. Cleota came into it with me, and Clem knows. They're about the only ones that really matter and I have no problems there. The adults understand fully.

"I do too."

Somehow that thought warmed Sarah's heart. She put her head on her knees. Her voice was muffled, "I'll be so glad when this is over."

Leaves fell from the tree, as Samuel shifted. He'd felt the impulse to reach for her, but caught himself in time.

"It won't be much longer. If this shipment works, we could be out of this much sooner than we'd thought possible. There would be no more need for us to stay here, if that happens," he said.

"I— don't know what I'll do when I go home." Her voice broke, "Daniel won't be there," slipped out.

He hesitated, "Who is Daniel?"

"He was my fiancée. Adkisson's bunch killed him."

"I am sorry. I didn't know that."

"No, not too many do. Our engagement was still se-cret, but Papa knew. Daniel worked at the iron works. He was carrying the payroll that they tried to steal. He gave his life to hold on to it for the men, but he died a few minutes after the attack. I got to him. He died in my arms, telling me that he wished we could have been together forever."

Silence came from above.

Sarah continued, more freely than if she had looked into another's face. "There's not really much one can say when someone loses one they love. I've been through it, about all you can do is be there."

"Was someone there?" Samuel asked.

"Not exactly. Papa was injured and he was almost entirely in bed until about the time we started our training. I couldn't unload on him. Cleota helped me. She was the only one that really understood."

"And now she's not around either."

"No— I'm sorry. Thanks for listening to me, since I can't see you, it's been like talking to myself, but it has helped," Sarah said.

"Thanks!" he said.

"For what?"

"For saying. talking to me is like talking to yourself."

"Oh, I didn't mean that the way it sounded." She started, then looked at the sky. "It's getting late, I'd better get back. I can't be away too long, something might happen. I don't want to miss anything after all the efforts we've put into this thing." Sarah rose and shook out her skirt.

"I'll be seeing you again before long. Don't forget, stay inside on Friday and off the streets," Samuel cautioned.

"Yes, I will. Take care of yourself."

"I always do," he said.

"That's what most of us think, but I've learned differently, we can't always. I'll be praying for you too," Sarah whispered.

"Keep up the good work and stay safe."

Sarah walked slowly away, seeming to admire the trees and the flowers in the cemetery. She took her time, appearing in no hurry and without a care, the aimless wandering of a young girl spending an afternoon daydreaming.

Samuel watched with a heavy heart, grieved for her.

For an hour he sat in his tree perch, then slipped down and away as dusk descended upon the quiet cemetery.

Samuel slipped into Clem's room during the night. No one was likely to be about during the middle hours. The two compared information and observations, then the conversation drifted to Sarah.

Clem thought a moment, "Let's arrange for Sarah to

see Cleota."

"Do you think we could?" Samuel asked.

"I think we could come up with a place that would be safe, and I think it would be good for them both. Where would you suggest?" Clem asked.

"I met her in the cemetery, but I was out of sight. I don't think that would do for Cleota. There are too many people visiting off and on."

"And there's too many directions to watch."

"How about the back room of the store?" Samuel asked.

"I don't know about that. My boss might come in and there are always people in the alleyway. Someone might stumble on them and put two and two together. I think this is too close to her old neighborhood," Clem said.

"Cleota isn't supposed to be in New Orleans. Maybe we could take Sarah somewhere else," Samuel said.

"Say, how about Henri's shrimp boat?" Clem asked.

"That might work. Maybe I could take Cleota to shop for shrimp, or she might hire on to clean the tank. We have people coming by every time we get in port, especially when we have a fresh catch."

"See if you can arrange it with Henri's," Clem said.

"They leave me on board sometimes, I'll volunteer and let them go home to supper," Samuel answered.

"Do you ever stay on board at night?"

"Sometimes, we have the catch iced down and stay on, if we haven't sold out."

"Figure out something. You make arrangements with Cleota and I'll get word to Sarah."

"I'll work on it," Samuel said.

"When do you think you'll be in port next time?"

"Should be in early Thursday, so the Catholics of New Orleans can have their fish on Friday."

"Let's plan it for late Thursday afternoon, when

customers have thinned out. Maybe we can arrange for Cleota and Sarah to be the only customers you have at that hour," Clem said.

"I could put up a *sold out* sign, if we're getting nearly empty."

"I wouldn't want to cheat Henri's out of any business, but you can see how your catch is going by then. Maybe I can rustle up a few extra buyers very early, so we can be sure you're sold out," Clem said.

"I'll make sure Cleota and Sarah take some home. I'll reserve the best before the catch is picked over," Samuel said.

"This is exciting. It sure is fun to do something nice for someone for a change."

"Don't you do nice things at the store all the time?"

"Sure, but nothing like this. I load feed, bring in the produce, polish the apples, sweep the floor— "

"I get it. But you do a few very important things too," Samuel added.

"I know and I'm glad those are far between. I'll be glad when I can move on to something more normal and use my education again," Clem said.

Sarah was talking about it in the cemetery the other day," Samuel replied.

"Her life is kind of hard," Clem agreed.

"I'd hate to live in that house without any close friends nearby and feel the presence of her enemy every day," Samuel added.

"Well, maybe this will help. It's about all we can do for her right now," Clem said.

"Yes, and be here, if she needs us."

"Right."

"Sam, make certain Cleota comes in disguise."

"She's got a big sunbonnet we provided. That should cover her face."

In anticipation of the *shipment*, on Friday, Sarah made sure the household was inside and kept busy with extra spring-cleaning. She meant to keep those in her charge safe. Briefly she spoke to Gideon, "You stay close in your lawn today, there's something going on in the city."

All day, she waited, but nothing happened.

Did the wrong people get word?

"You're nervous as a cat, is somethin' wrong?" Josie asked after her second thwarted attempt to go to the market.

"No, I just want all this done before Easter. No time like the present, they always say." Sarah made a resolve to stay away from those who knew her best. She had no desire to have anyone guess she knew what was about to happen in the city. That could be dangerous for all of them.

The day crept on. The sun went down, the household went to its rest. Sarah sat in a chair in her room. *I'd like to talk to Clem. Wonder if he's still up? I can't risk it after he told me to stay home. I can't be on the streets at night. He may be involved in something and I'd mess it up. Stay calm!*

Dear Lord, calm my soul, give me patience to deal with whatever comes. She laid her head back on the chair and drifted off to sleep. Toward morning she roused enough to get into her bed.

She prayed as she adjusted the netting on her four-poster, *Well, Lord you gave me patience and I guess I needed it. It's almost morning and nothing has happened. I don't guess it will now. Whatever happens, You deal with it, I'm going to get a little sleep before morning.*

The next morning, she cleared her work at home, then went to Fuqua's. When she found Clem alone, she inquired, "Clem, what happened?"

"I'm sorry that I couldn't get you word, but there were complications and the shipment didn't come."

"I kept everyone busy all day. They finally got almost

angry with me. If this happens again, I think maybe you shouldn't tell me ahead of time. If I was this nervous, I might let something slip out."

"They probably won't tell me next time either. I was sharp with customers all day, hurrying them in and out. Mr. Fuqua finally told me to go to my room and he'd take care of business. I think he was afraid I'd run off all his customers."

"I don't even want to know what was supposed to happen. I might have a nightmare, talk in my sleep, or something," Sarah admitted.

"Yes, I can understand what you're saying."

The two laughed together.

"I guess we ought to be more serious. I doubt it was a laughing matter," she said.

"I expect you're right, but we can chalk it up to nervous relief this time. Guess we're entitled to that once in a while," Clem observed.

"That's for sure, it's been kind of tense around here lately. I need to get on back, I'll be seeing you next time."

"Bye for now." Clem gazed after her as she walked down the street.

Mr. Fuqua came through the storeroom door. "You moonin' after that girl, Clem?"

Clem ducked his head, caught in his staring.

"Spose so, she's nice and I do like her."

"She's a little young for you, Son. She'd make a good baby sister, but you'd better pick on someone your own age." He scratched under his beard, "Maybe I shouldn't have said that, sometimes young girls do marry older fellows. My wife is younger'n me and we've always been happy."

Clem had to stop himself from voicing his thoughts. *She's older than you think and exactly the right age for me.*

Reunion

The ring of Yankees continued to close more tightly around the city. Food and produce became more and more scarce. In hopes she'd catch a new shipment, Sarah checked often on Fuqua's latest offerings. Added to their own efforts with their kitchen garden and substitution, the household continued to exist without painful scarcity.

They had enough to satisfy barest requirements but each longed for their favorites, some food they had previously taken for granted.

Clem grinned when he saw Sarah. He spoke for her ears only, "Sarah, I got word, you're to go to Henri's shrimper at six this Thursday evening. A carriage will call for you at your house."

"That's late. How do you know it will be safe?" she asked.

"I'll send someone for you. It will be above reproach. You needn't worry about your reputation," Clem said.

"I wasn't worried about my reputation, but I was worried about appearances for other reasons," she added.

"It will be all right. We've seen to that. Tell the servants at Adkisson's that you're going to visit a sick friend."

"I don't have any friends here and they know it."

"Tell them it is Mrs. Henri. I'll see that she agrees and we'll get the word passed that she is ailing. You've met her when you bought shrimp."

"I have?"

"Don't you remember, of course you have!" he grinned.

"I see. I'll be ready and I'll take her some soup to make it even more of a reality."

"They'll see you Thursday, and I want a full report as soon as you can get back to me," he added.

"You look suspicious, has this all been cleared?" Sarah asked.

"Would I take a chance if it hadn't been?"

At precisely six, Thursday evening, a hired city carriage appeared outside the front gate, at the end of the shell walkway.

Sarah was ready. She turned from the front hallway, opened the kitchen door and spoke to Josie,

"I'm not certain how soon I'll be back. My friends have assured me I'll have an escort, so don't worry if it gets late."

"Yes, Ma'am, but what if Mr. Adkisson returns and wants you to write for him?"

"Tell him his messages are on his desk, and I'll see him in the morning if he has correspondence he wishes to get out."

"You've never been gone before, what if he doesn't like it?" Josie asked.

"He doesn't hire me, so I'm sure he will agree that I do have some personal time to myself. He seldom wishes me to work after early afternoon." She hurriedly stepped out the open door and closed it behind her. *I'm fearful the young master might return and prevent my excursion. I feel quivery inside. Wonder what's coming about? Prepare me Lord, and be with this, help me deal with it, whatever it is.*

The ride to the docks was a nice change for Sarah. Seldom had she been out in the city since she had been there as a child with her father. As they passed, memories bore in upon her; memories of her and her father having good times; memories of seeing the sights of the city; and memories of early costume galas. Memories of parties, most thought her too young to attend. Tears came and ran unchecked down her face.

The quietness of the carriage brought her back to reality. *Where am I? I was so engrossed in my memories that I've missed where I have traveled.*

The door on the carriage was thrown open and Samuel reached his hand into the dark interior to take Sarah's hand in his. She drew back and fumbled for her handkerchief.

"Sarah— are you all right? It's me, Samuel. I'm here to get you."

Her handkerchief muffled her voice. "Ye-es, I'm fine. I was lost in my memories and didn't realize I'd arrived."

"That's fine, you just got here. Your driver hasn't alighted," he aid.

"I'm sorry I was so engrossed, I didn't intend to ignore you."

"Come inside." He whispered in her ear, "We've got a surprise for you!"

He turned back to the carriage, "Driver, she'll be a while but I'll make it worth your wait."

"Yes, Suh."

Samuel helped her from the carriage. The driver alighted to tie his team to the small black iron jockey with the large ring in his hand.

Samuel took Sarah's elbow and moved her hurriedly toward the door of the fish shack.

"I can hardly see after the darkness of the carriage. Are we in a hurry?" she asked.

"We are, or at least I am! I think you will be too when you see the surprise."

Sarah blinked as they came into the dim light of the fish shack. The place smelled of the day's catch, and perhaps the catch of other days as well. She wrinkled her nose.

"You get used to the smell after while, but when you first come in, it's rather strong." He guided her toward the back. "Your surprise is over here."

Cleota appeared from behind the canvas door covering. She squealed as she lumbered toward Sarah, who just in time opened her arms. The pair fell together, mingling their tears.

Cleota patted the child she had mothered most of her adult life.

"There, there, honey. It's so good to see you."

"And I, you, but seeing you is so much better than only hearing about you," Sarah said.

"I been hearing about you from this boy. He's a good one."

"Yes," Sarah said.

Samuel teased, "I'm a good one, or you been hearing about me?"

Cleota answered for both of them, "A good one, *and* hearing about you."

The two women fell together, renewing their sobbing and laughing together in their combined joy.

Samuel motioned to the pair. "Sit over here. I covered a couple of kegs for your visit. I'll go back to work and you can visit. You can tell me when you're ready to go, or I'll come back, at the latest, by nine."

"Samuel, maybe you better give this soup to Mrs. Henri. I don't want to have to lie about making the soup for her. Tell her I'll speak to her after our visit, if that suits her."

"I'll see that you get to meet her again. Don't want you fibbing." Samuel went out the door with Sarah's soup pail in his hands.

Cleota spoke first, "How are you? Has that Asden bothered you anymore?"

"No, in fact, I think he's out of town now. He came by and left a message for Mr. Adkisson and said he was leaving town."

"How did he act when you saw him?"

"I think he was a little embarrassed. He never did tell Mr. Adkisson what happened. He probably recalled he was out of line and drunk.

"Did you tell Adkisson?"

"Not really. I think he knew something happened. He didn't want to condemn his friend, so he just ignored it and had me move you. He didn't seem to want to deal with the problem. He's never mentioned it since."

"I'm glad it didn't get you in trouble. Are things going along with the shipments?"

"I don't know much. Something was supposed to happen that didn't, but I never knew what. I don't think I want to know. That way, I don't have to worry about letting something slip."

Cleota nodded, "Yes, it is confusing. I hear little rumblin's, but I don't really find out much."

"Just as well. That way, we won't tell stories accidentally. Should something really bad happen, we don't know anything to tell. I do pass on what I get, but I don't understand much of it. I only get bits and pieces and I don't know how useful some of it is," Sarah said.

"Let's talk about somethin' else for once. How are you, really?" Cleota asked.

"I'm fine." She hugged Cleota again. "I can't tell you how much I've missed you. I'll be so glad when we can be together again and all this is over."

"You found any handsome young man yet?"

"Where would I meet a handsome young man that isn't the enemy?" Sarah asked.

"Samuel? Clem?'

"We hardly meet under good circumstances for getting to know one another. Anyway, they make really good brothers and that's all we can be now," Sarah said.

"Brothers can be friends. Friends become lovers."

"Cleota!" Sarah huffed.

"Well, we saw it happen once with Daniel."

"Yes, he was a wonderful friend, *first*." Sarah looked away as tears brimmed again.

"Oh, Honey. I didn't mean to make you sad again."

"You didn't. Tonight, I seem ready to cry every minute. Too many things happening, I guess. I'm not accustomed to things anymore."

Before the ladies were ready, Samuel came into the fish shack.

"Sarah, Mrs. Henri is ready to see you now. Come inside and I'll introduce you."

He turned and spoke quietly, "Cleota, it's time to go now. Here's a package of shrimp. Hope you can enjoy it. The youngest Henri is ready to walk you home. You can go first. We shouldn't all leave at once."

"Good night, Sarah." Cleota hugged her again. "Thank you Samuel. You don't know what this has meant to us. You're a good man." Cleota patted his arm and looked at Sarah. She turned, looked back one last time, smiled, then disappeared out the canvas door in the rear.

Samuel took Sarah's arm and moved her toward a side door.

ຂ໋

After her visit to mother Henri, Samuel put Sarah into the carriage and got in beside her.

Sarah was surprised when he sat next to her. "Are you going too?"

"Wouldn't miss it. I often go to see Clem at night. He gets lonely all by himself in his loft over the store."

"I can imagine."

"Imagine what?"

"That Clem might get lonely."

Samuel turned toward Sarah. His knee brushed her thigh. In his intensity, he didn't notice, but Sarah did.

"Sarah, do you get lonely in that big house with all the people?"

"Yes, because as you know, there is no one I can really talk to there."

"Like the Henris. *Pull in the nets, clean the tanks. Work talk.*"

"Yes," she said.

"We've got a half hour, the driver can't hear, unload fast," Samuel encouraged.

"I hate to always fill your ears with my problems."

"I really don't mind. In fact, it actually gives me something else to think about and I enjoy hearing your voice."

"You can't really mean that?" Sarah said.

"Yes, I can. If this is ever over, I plan to make you believe that."

Sarah tried to read his face. "What do you mean by what you just said?"

"I mean that you interest me and I plan to court you, when we're free to be ourselves." He reached for her hand. His warm fingers curled around her small hand. He placed her hand between his two and rubbed his fingers over her suddenly, very cold hand.

"Give me your other hand. Is it as cold as this one?" he asked.

Sarah did not pull her hand away, but gave him her other too. She enjoyed the closeness of the carriage and the safety she suddenly felt.

She didn't look out at the city as they passed, but the two made small talk.

"We're almost there," Samuel whispered above the sound of the carriage wheels.

"This is peaceful. I wish it didn't have to end."

"I don't either, but— back to our lives."

"They aren't real pleasant, are they?" Sarah asked.

"No, but I can assure you, life *will* be good again."

"I'll remember that promise. Do you always keep your word?"

"Do you?" Samuel said.

"You know I do, other than for this job."

She shifted, "I have to suit our purposes, as do you."

"But not much longer," he said.

Samuel raised her hands to his lips and brushed a kiss across the back of one hand. Sarah could not see his face to read the meaning of his actions.

The carriage stopped. He stepped out and reached for Sarah's hand.

"Thank you Samuel, I'll be forever grateful for your kindness."

Samuel spoke to the driver. "Wait and I'll be right back." He walked her to the front porch, reached for her hand and squeezed it again. Then, he waited until she was in and he heard the door click.

Sarah leaned against the door, then turned to peep out the side light and watch Samuel walk back to the carriage.

"You're rather late!" a masculine voice spoke from the darkness.

Sarah jumped. "Oh! I didn't know anyone was still awake?" She could see the red ash on Mr. Adkisson's cigar. *If I'd been less starry-eyed, I'd have smelled his cigar.*

"Yes, I got back about dark and the cook said you had gone to visit a sick friend. Was that the one?" he asked.

"No, one of her sons saw me home safely. They didn't want me to come alone," she explained.

"Surely," he dismissed her. "You'd better get some rest, we have work tomorrow."

"Yes, Sir." Sarah fled before he could make other comments, or ask further questions.

I feel guilty again. Why do I let myself feel this way? Like I was doing something wrong, and I'm not. I went to see a friend and I— found another friend. What's wrong with that? He sounded angry. Why? I'm going to be happy and enjoy tonight, no matter what— or who.

୧ᕊ·

When Sarah returned to the store, Clem seemed more intense than usual.

"You seem worried. Is there something I should know?" she asked.

He sighed, "Yes, but it's personal."

She looked at him intently and he returned her scrutiny. "Have you had bad news from home?"

"No. Walk out front with me and I'll tell you."

"You're scaring me. Is it something bad?"

"I don't know. You tell me?" he stated.

"How can I, I don't know what you're talking about."

"Oh, sorry, of course you don't. Let's walk a bit."

"Are you sure you want to be seen with me?" she asked.

"Oh, but I do want to be seen with you. You see Samuel told me that he planned to court you when this is over." He turned to look into her face, "I intend to do the same."

She considered the warm feeling in her chest and spoke quietly. "Clem, you both shock me. How can you even think about courting in times like this? I have trouble keeping my head on straight, much less thinking about a future of *any* kind, with *any one*."

"Maybe that's why we are thinking about courting. Time may be very short and this may be our only opportunity. Many soldiers are marrying their girls before they go off to war. Our circumstances aren't much different."

"Well, I have to tell you both, I can't think about courting right now. I do love you both, but—" She looked quickly at Clem when she heard his indrawn breath. "Let me finish. I love you as brothers and co-workers. I'm sorry, but I've got all I can handle now. Please don't complicate our lives by competing, or demanding more from me than I can give. We need to keep clear heads, or we could all die, like Daniel did."

"I guess you're more mature than us, but we seem to be caught up in the urgency of the moment. You are thinking more clearly than either of us. I'm sorry I've troubled you."

"You haven't troubled me, and I'm glad you're both my friends. But now you know how I feel. Can we drop it and go back to being just friends, at least for the time being?"

"Sure, but don't expect us to remain neutral when this thing is over," Clem promised.

She smiled at Clem. "I will hold you to your word, just as I do Samuel. He made me a promise too. I'll hold both of you to your word when things settle down, *and* we've all got normal lives again."

"Thank you, Sarah."

"You both make me very grateful to have such good friends. It's hard to believe that we have found each other amidst the hazards that have surrounded us."

"I won't embarrass you again by bringing it up, but I couldn't let ole Sam get ahead of me, now could I?"

"Guess not." She poked Clem on the arm with her index finger, "Now keep quiet, you hear?"

They grinned and turned back toward the store, friends again. *Friends with promise.*

On the way home, Sarah felt a warmth centered in her heart.

Lord, You know what I need and all this makes me feel less alone.

On her loneliest nights, Sarah took out the promises and savored them. The two men's expressions of feeling brought a warmth of safety and love, even though she felt none of them was free to act on their friendship.

❦

Asden met Adkisson at the edge of the swamp. "Someone knows our plans. It must be someone in your acquaintance."

"I can't imagine who, but it seems that way."

"Check that girl who does your correspondence— she's involved more than any other one person."

"I don't think— " Montgomery interrupted.

"Test her. Here, I've fixed a message. I put some numbers and places in it. If she takes the letter, opens it, or gives it to someone, then we'll know for sure."

"I don't like this!"

"You don't have a choice," Asden said.

"All right, if you insist. I'll lay the trap and watch to see if it's sprung."

That afternoon, Adkisson made a display of placing the message on his desk.

"I have a letter here for the messenger. He'll be here Wednesday this week. It's very important that this goes out." He fumbled with his cane.

"Are you well, Sir?"

"I was deciding if I'd go out tonight. Yes, I think I shall. I won't be in until very late."

"Yes, sir." Sarah ducked her head in acceptance.

After dusk, he placed himself outside the house. He crouched below his office window. Soon the household settled for the night. He let himself stealthily into his office through the raised window. When inside, he closed and latched the window. Adkisson scooted down into the huge recess under his desk.

At midnight, he heard a soft swishing sound. First the front door rattled, the sound came nearer, almost upon him. He could see Sarah's form before the window. She checked the latch and left the room. He heard her go to the back door, then heard the stairs creak as she ascended the back way to her room. He listened until he heard the door overhead shut, and then the clink of the water pitcher upon her washbowl. *Locking up, that's all.*

He slipped his head above the top of his desk. The white envelope lay just as he had left it in the moonlight coming through the window.

He let out a breath and eased to sit in his chair. He slumped and lighted a cigar.

After his cigar burned low, he stretched out on the leather sofa and soon slept.

Very early, he heard Sarah and the servants as they arose and began their morning work. He straightened his vest, put on his coat and sat down at his desk.

"I knew she was harmless, now Asden will believe me," he muttered under his breath.

"Sarah, come here!"

"Yes, sir?"

"Take a letter please. It's to Lawrence Asden. You know the address."

"I've completed my efforts— all's well. Proceed as planned. I'll be meeting you on the eighth. Then put on the proper signatures and give it to the messenger tonight along with the one on the desk."

Sarah did as she was bidden. After Montgomery left the house, relief flooded over her.

Lord, You were right as you always are. I feel that statement, "I've completed my effort," was a trap for me and thanks to you, I didn't take the bait. Please don't let him become more suspicious. I've got so much to do here. Protect us all. Thank you, Amen.

Sarah hurried to the store as early as would be seemly in the morning. When she arrived, she waited until Clem was alone.

"I think Mr. Adkisson is suspicious," she blurted.

"Why do you think that?" he asked.

"He put a message on his desk and called my attention to it. I thought it was important, but he said he was going to be out until late."

"What did you do?"

"I intended to look at it, but God seemed to me."

"How did He do that?" Clem asked.

"I heard a voice say, *Leave it*. It was clear as you and me talking," she replied.

"And you did?"

"Yes, and I'm pretty sure he watched last night."

"Did you see him?"

"No, but I could sense he was there somewhere in the room. The window was locked when I checked it and the front door was locked this morning. I don't think he came in after I checked the locks," she explained.

"Surely there would be no place to hide in that room," Clem suggested.

"When I checked the windows and doors at midnight, I caught the gleam of his gold cane. It was setting where he always puts it when he's home."

"Maybe he forgot it last night?"

"No. I saw him pick it up when he said he was going out. It's a sword. He never goes out without it and it was in the same place this morning while he was sitting at his desk."

"You may be right. Sarah? Please be careful."

"There's more. He wrote Asden a message this morning and he said, "I've completed my effort, all's well. Proceed as planned. I'll meet you on the eighth.""

"That's all?"

"Yes, but I felt there was meaning between the lines."

"That could be," Clem said.

"I think I was being tested and I passed this time," she said.

"I'm thinking you should not pass on any message you don't hear or write yourself. I don't think we should try to open any for a while. It's getting more and more risky, the closer our people come."

"Yes, I think they've become suspicious of everyone. I hope it's a good sign," Sarah sighed.

"I do too. We're about there, Sarah."

"I'm so glad."

"We can't let down just yet. Keep your eyes and ears open, but, Sarah— "

"What?"

Clem touched her arm, "Take care of yourself, we can't have anything happen to you now."

Decisions, Decisions?

Lawrence Asden rushed into the house when Samson opened the door. He stomped directly to the young master's study.

Overhearing the commotion, the young master reached for his cane, his chair fell over backwards, as he rose. When he saw Lawrence, he turned to sit the chair on its legs.

"Oh! Come in, Lawrence. What's the matter?"

"You're blamed right, I've come here to plan getting rid of a viper in our midst!"

The young master closed the door to the study. Sarah crept as close as she dared with her dust mop in her hand. The voices were loud. She need not press her ear to the door.

Asden spoke abruptly, "That man you placed in my company has betrayed us all and I mean to dispose of him."

Sarah could not hear the young master's reply, immediately followed by Asden's roar.

"I *will* be rid of him. He's out of town for two days, but I will catch him enroute. He'll never return to this city!"

"Now, now. What makes you think he has betrayed you?"

"I was looking for writing material and found one of my supply orders taped to the underside of his drawer. He's the only one privy to these munitions orders. Someone knows too much about our operations and with this evidence. I've found a spy!"

"If he were going to reveal your order, surely he would have carried the list away to the enemy."

"It doesn't matter. His usefulness to me has ended. I'll never trust him again."

"Why don't you set a trap for him like I did and see what he does with some false information?"

"And to think, I treated him like a son."

"Think about it, he's been very valuable to you and he was here, long before we had any trouble with those northern imports."

"I'll think about a trap. But I can't imagine anyone else carrying information from my warehouse."

Sarah heard the scrap of the study chair and the squeak of Mr. Adkisson's chair as he rose. She backed to the end of the hallway and began dusting the floor toward the back door. Her back was to the study door as someone fumbled for the door and it swung open.

Asden cast a quick glance in her direction and muttered, "Lurking, always lurking, people are always lurking about in this city anymore."

"Now Lawrence, settle down or you're going to make yourself sick again."

Asden stomped to the front door, jerked it open, exited and slammed it after himself.

Sarah looked after him.

"Sarah, come here," commanded the young master.

"Yes, Sir."

"My friend was rather agitated, did you overhear?"

Sarah's heart lurched. She looked at the young master. *No one could avoid overhearing. Honesty would be best here.*

"A few muffled words," she said.

He looked at her sharply, then turned away. "Fine, it was nothing, go on about your business."

Sarah turned and dusted unhurriedly up the stairway.

I must get this message to my contact as quickly as possible. I don't dare go to Clem tonight and Gideon would be in danger, if I contact him. I'll carry it to the cemetery myself and place it between the stones. I'll have to wait until darkness comes, or Mr. Adkisson might be suspicious. In case this clerk is one of ours, he must be warned and I'll have to do it.

Nearing bedtime, in hopes of passing time more quickly, she rocked in the chair sitting on the rug in front of the window where she could see who came and went in the street outside. Agitated and unable to sit, she rose and paced the floor. She removed her shoes so she would not make undue noise.

There are a few streaks of lightning, rain will make the sky darker than usual and less agreeable to be outside in a storm. Perhaps it will keep my enemy in too. Thank you Lord.

She heard the front door shut, then observed the young master strolling up the front path with his cloak over his arm.

Soon— I'll be able to slip out the back way very soon.

She gathered her cape, encrypted the information about a suspected informant in Mr. Asden's company who was out of town for the next two days. She folded the message into a tiny square, creased the edges tightly and put it into the bottom of her skirt pocket with her derringer.

He's been gone half an hour, usually he doesn't come back for hours, I should have time and it is dark. No one can see me.

Sarah folded her cape into a small bundle and went quietly down the servant's stairs toward the door onto the back verandah. She listened before she entered the kitchen. All was quiet. She slipped from the house and paused in the shadow of the magnolia tree to listen, then put on her cape. She pulled the hood over her hair and down over her face and hurried to the cemetery.

The lightning purged. Rain began to slash beneath her hood into her face. She increased her pace until she almost ran. Quietly she edged along the shadows of the brick wall surrounding the cemetery and slipped through the tiny opening between the two iron gates. The chain allowed enough space for her small frame to squeeze through.

As she reached to place her message into the crevice in the tombstone, she heard a sound. She pressed herself against the gray stone and stilled her breathing. The lightning flashed. Sarah saw she was not alone.

Immediately after the next flash, she slipped quickly to the next stone and crouched behind it. Awaiting the next flash, she looked back to see the man casting about in the cemetery. With each blast of lightning and the following thunder she sought to put distance between them. Once she caught the man looking full at her. A blaze of lightning lit, *Lawrence Asden's face.*

Does he suspect me; am I the informant of which he spoke? I've got to get away from him. He's very dangerous to our mission.

Again the lightning flashed. Counting on her adversary's momentary blindness, she moved further toward a gate that she'd observed on one of her trips to the cemetery.

He's lost me, but I need to destroy this message in case I'm caught. Careful not to drop the tiniest particle, she began to shred the note into the finest pieces she could manage. She dipped the torn page into the first puddle she saw and shredded more, moving after each flash of lightning to put the next tombstone between herself and her pursuer.

Finally, she reached the gate. Her coat had become drenched and heavy. She was unable to squeeze her heavily clothed body between the bars. The chain clanked. She heard Asden running. Sarah drew back into the shadows inside the cemetery wall and waited. He came to the gate, pressed his face against the bars and peered in every direction.

Quickly, the large figure turned and ran back into the cemetery toward his horse. Hidden in the shadows, on the other side of the small cemetery, Sarah waited long enough to be sure he was going away, then pressed bits of the message into the soft dirt around a recent grave and smoothed each finger mark. She pressed another tiny particle into the base of a tree, one in the soft earth under a bush, some into a puddle and pressed down with her hand in the mud.

When she was rid of the tell tale evidence, she squeezed herself between the bars of the gate closest to the mansion. She sped home as quickly as she could, deposited her wet cape in the tack room of the coach house, ran through the garden, slipped into the mansion, barred the back door and crept up the stairs.

She peeled wet clothes from her body with cold clumsy fingers that wouldn't work. Hastily, she shoved them down onto the rug, then the whole pile under the bed, wrapped her hair in a towel and slipped on her robe. Shivering, she tried to rub some warmth into her arms and face. Her breath came in short gasps of fear and exertion. She poured water into the bowl and washed her hands.

Her breathing slowed, then she heard the clatter of a horse in the street in front of the house. In a moment, pounding sounded on the front door.

Samson shuffled up the hallway and questioned the visitor through the heavy door.

"Let me in, I need to talk to your housekeeper!"

"Who's there?"

"Lawrence Asden. Let me in or your master will hear about this!"

The old butler opened the door and Asden threw it back against the wall, knocking the old man off balance.

Sarah answered from her room in a sleepy voice.

"What is it Samson?"

"Mr. Asden to see you, Ma'am."

Sarah grabbed her nightcap, placed it on her head, stepped through the door and onto the landing at the top of the stairs. She put her hand to her mouth in a feigned yawn.

"Mr. Asden, it is very late for you to come calling. I won't come down. If you have something for Mr. Adkisson, lay it on the table and I'll get it after you leave."

Asden blustered. He huffed, "Nothing, it was nothing.

I'll see Montgomery tomorrow."

The man swirled from the front hallway. Samson closed the front door in his wake.

"I'll wipe the floor, Ma'am."

"Check the bolt. I'm going back to bed, good night. Thank you, Samson."

She turned into her room, quietly closed the door and leaned against it. She clutched at her chest and caught her breath on a sob.

I didn't get the message to my contacts, but I think it was another trap. This is one night that prayer is all I can do. I'll tell Clem tomorrow. I hope that poor clerk is safe and it was a false alarm. Maybe that will be in time. He said the clerk would be gone for several days. Please Lord.

Sarah fell across her bed and buried her face in her pillow. *I can't cry, I can't cry, please Lord.*

When she managed to calm herself, she began to pray for the safety of everyone involved in her mission.

She had a last thought before she slept, *I must put out a wash tomorrow to cover the wet clothes under my bed.*

Early the next day, Sarah sent Gideon to get flour for the household. She gave him verbal information for Clem.

"Don't tell Clem until there is no one else in the store, then tell him this. The man who sometimes comes to the house thinks there is a traitor amongst his warehouse employees, but he followed me last night He didn't see me. I'm fine and he went away. He didn't catch me. He's looking for a young man who has been gone for two days. He thinks this man is giving information on- " *I can't tell Gideon too much, in case he's says the wrong thing-* "to his enemy."

She looked away, "Whistle as soon as you return. I'll know you are back. If you have a return message, whistle twice and I'll come to the clothesline to check the wash."

I'm glad the sun is shining today.

The day dragged slowly for Sarah. Other than Gideon's single bird call, she received no further messages.

Lord, Please get them there in time.

April, 1862
New Orleans Under Siege

In the early hours of darkness two weeks later, the air and ground thumped with the solid impact of long distance cannon and artillery from the forts along the river. The sounds seemed to come from every direction.

Cries of alarm went out.

"They can't get by the forts," went round the town.

"They've taken all our able-bodied soldiers to Vicksburg and other points of this war," a citizen complained fearfully.

"They've left us with few defenses. If the Union ships get by the forts, we can't defend all these old people and children," the city wailed. "Gather everyone with a gun to help us defend the city."

Sarah was startled awake by the window vibrations.

The ships are coming from the Gulf. New Orleans is finally under siege. How long will it take? Lord, keep us safe. Keep everyone in the city safe and end it soon. We're in your hands. Thank God, Thank God! This is almost over, at least for us here!

The household literally wrung their hands the livelong day. War noises came closer and closer. The house vibrated with the booms.

Sarah reassured the household with her calm. Josie cried and Sarah reminded her of God's promise, "I have not given you a spirit of fear."

"I know Missy, but I can't help it!"

"Let's all gather in the kitchen and pray."

"What's gonna happen to us?"

"The Lord says he will supply all our needs. The kitchen is probably the safest place in the house. No, maybe the cellar is safer. Do you want to go down there Josie?"

"Yes 'em."

"All right, you stand on the steps, the rest of us will sit in the kitchen and pray."

Sarah and the five servants gathered around the kitchen worktable. The servants were too fearful to pray. Sarah started. Soon Samson took up a spirited "Amen" and the others joined in.

In the fervency of their prayer, they forgot their fear.

After they finished, Sarah gave them duties.

"Mostly, I want you to stay in this room. If the house should catch fire, we'll need water from the cistern. I'll get buckets from the coach house; fill them from the cistern; then line them up on the back verandah."

Sarah left and was soon back filling buckets. She struggled with a brimming bucket in each hand.

Samson was shamed and rushed to take the last two from her.

Breathlessly, Sarah said, "Put them under the work bench. If we need to drink or wash, they'll be ready."

"Yes, Ma'am."

"Now let's sit a spell. Josie are there any potatoes down there to peel?"

"Yes 'em."

"Pass them up, let's keep our hands busy."

⚜

Montgomery Adkisson rushed into the house, searched until he heard voices from the kitchen. He opened the door, took the astonished Sarah's arm. He lifted her from her chair. They left the shocked household servants sitting at the table, more fearful than ever.

With his hand at her back, he guided her ahead of him, and out onto the verandah at the back of the house. He didn't speak until he was out of the servants' hearing.

"Lovell has surrendered the whole city to the Yanks, but you're coming along with me. Not every rat hole is closed, we can still get out. I've learned some things about you that I didn't know before. I'm taking you for added protection!"

Sarah's heart lurched. "What do you mean?"

He hissed into her ear, "I got a message from *your friend*, Mr. Asden. Since you know so much, you must be a Yankee spy. As such, you may be very valuable to me." He grabbed her arm and hauled her to his side, "Come along. Don't give me any trouble!"

She muffled her scream, but it echoed through the garden.

Gideon's scared face peered through the fence. When he saw Sarah being dragged along by the young master, he hurried to the loose dirt of a ground hog hole, pushed the dirt away from the heavy bars and wiggled under. He rose and yelled, "Miss Sarah?"

Sarah thought fast. "Go home, Gideon. It's fine, I just saw a mouse and it startled me."

"No, missy, I know youse got troubles."

Adkisson shoved her ahead of him. "Okay, boy. Come here, if you don't want your friend hurt."

"Please don't take him, he's just a helpless child," Sarah pleaded.

Noises came from the street in front of the house. Blue-clad troops advancing throughout the city met no resistance.

"Sarah, I'll blow his head off, if you say one word or reveal our escape! I'll just take your little slave pet along too. Come on boy!"

"Sarah grunted and dragged down on Adkisson's arm, "Run, Gideon, get away!"

Adkisson struck at her, the blow glanced off her arm. Gideon leaped like a terrier and clung to the upraised arm. The man struck with his cane. He knocked the boy down. Gideon fell dazed and bleeding.

Sarah reached for the boy.

"Come on, or I'll kill him right here!" He jerked her arm.

Gideon is better off here—unconscious. Please Lord, let someone find him, care for him. Help me handle this— help our men catch this evil man who plotted so many things in the past months. Make him pay for all the hurt he has given others, including my family and Daniel. It's me and him, and You Lord. May your will be done.

Calm settled on Sarah's spirit. She turned her face reluctantly from Gideon and walked quietly along with Adkisson to the stables.

"Come along, I've still got my horse. I'm getting out of town and you're going with me."

"I'm surprised you still have your horse. The others have been gone for a long while."

"It pays to have friends in high places."

Adkisson tightened the saddle girth and laced a bag of provisions in front of the saddle.

"I know you're not properly dressed for a horseback ride, but get on behind the saddle." He watched her struggle to reach the stirrup.

She sensed he was afraid to let her go long enough to get aboard. He hesitated.

"Can you lead him to that block? I can't reach the stirrup," she stated.

"I'll give you a lift." He cupped his hands and she placed her left foot into his hands. She scrambled on behind the saddle and spread her skirts modestly.

"I'm coming up." He mounted and gathered the reins in his left hand. He gripped her arm at his waist with his right, "Don't give me any trouble, or you'll be very sorry."

He rode to the arched door of the carriage house and looked up and down the street. They slipped out on the loaded horse and rode quietly down the darkening street.

Adkisson had long planned his escape. He knew the back streets well. They took the most deserted roads away from the populated portions of the city and skirted the incoming troops from the great river. Sarah felt they went west, even though she was thoroughly confused.

She fidgeted. *I should jump before he gets away from all these people.*

He tightened his grip on the wrist he now held at the right side of his waist.

"Don't even think of giving me trouble. I could snap your arm like a match stick if you tried anything."

Sarah's hand lost feeling where the circulation was shut down. She wiggled her fingers.

"You can let up, I can't feel my fingers any longer."

"Promise me you won't jump," he snarled.

Sarah put her head down. A tear trickled down her cheek.

Adkisson turned and looked into her face. His face softened and he unwound his fingers from her small wrist.

She didn't answer him.

୬୶

Somehow, during the night, they left the city behind them. As dawn came, they holed up in a deserted warehouse along the river.

They spent a restless day in the hot building. After sunset, they roused and traveled in silence. At midnight, Adkisson began to talk.

"I know about you working with the Yankees. Why did you betray me? I never did anything to you."

Sarah had nothing to say.

They traveled through the night in silence.

Adkisson asked again, "Why did you betray me? I was kind and never hurt you."

At first she was reluctant to talk about her losses, but she calmed and began her story. "But you did hurt me seriously."

"In what way?"

"Your men crippled my father and wounded my uncle."

"I don't believe you know what you're saying."

"Oh, but I do. Do *you* remember when your hirelings tried to rob the payroll from Turner Iron Works in St. Louis?"

He gasped. "That wasn't me."

"No, but since we're being honest. I know it was your men."

"How did you come by that information?"

"Your henchmen mentioned getting money for *Adkisson's war effort*. One of the victims heard them," Sarah breathed quietly.

"Who? What did you say?"

Sarah continued, speaking quietly, "Yankees have a very good system for gaining information. They found out all about it, even before my father's fever left, they gave us more information as to your whereabouts and your whole operation."

Sarah looked away, "You injured my uncle too."

"Well, I'm sorry if your father was hurt and your Uncle. It didn't do us much good," he spoke bitterly.

She spoke almost to herself, "When people seek to do evil, it doesn't do anyone much good." She was quiet for a few minutes, reflecting on the conflicts she found in this man. *He can kill others; mistreat slaves, yet he treats me— decently. A southern gentleman, I think not.*

"I hear your Yankee accent now," he commented.

"I don't have to hide it from you any longer."

᷿

They rode in silence for hours.

"How did you come to be in the house I leased?"

"Seceding areas are falling, I no longer see a problem in revealing some of my part," Sarah spoke softly without emotion.

"Go ahead, I'd be most interested in hearing your

story."

"That was set up, long before you moved into the house. You were advised and led in that direction. I was in place and ready when you arrived. I have friends in high places too."

"I could hate you for what you've done!" he snarled.

"Actually, I almost hated you when you first came there, that's what motivated me to help. As time passed, I've started praying for you."

"You've what?" he exclaimed.

"I started praying for you."

"I don't know why you would do that."

"When one follows Jesus' example, it is difficult not to love your enemies."

"It isn't hard for me to hate my enemies," he said.

"That's human nature, to hate one's enemies, but that's not what God demands of us. I hate what you did, but not *you*, as one of God's creations."

"I'm not one of God's creations, I made myself!"

"Hardly. There's no way that you could create yourself, you didn't give birth to yourself did you?"

She heard him grind his teeth, unable to answer such logic.

The night passed in riding and hiding.

By dawn, they were well concealed in a gully overrun with brush. During that day, the horse browsed where he was tied to the bushes in the undergrowth.

Still unbelieving, Adkisson asked Sarah again why she had involved herself in the business of spying.

She picked up their conversation from the night before. "There's even more reason why I should hate you."

"What's that?"

"The carrier of the payroll was my fiancée," she spoke quietly, her voice caught.

"You're too young to have a fiancée!"

"I'm twenty-three."

"You couldn't be. They told me you were fourteen and a half when I rented the house. You don't look it— why you've acted an adolescent girl!"

"That's right, like you said, I *acted* the part," she agreed.

A look of speculation, then admiration touched Adkisson's face.

"I have to say you did a good job of it. I never once caught you in anything suspicious. Maybe Asden did. I don't know why, but he was always suspicious."

"Yes, I think he became so, but I don't know why. Perhaps some people look for traits in others, they have in themselves. Maybe suspicion grows suspicion." Sarah looked toward the setting sun shining through the bushes.

"Were there others involved," Adkisson questioned?

"I won't tell you that."

"I'd be a fool to think you worked alone."

"Perhaps."

"You had to get information to someone and receive from someone," he stated.

"You can assume anything you wish, but I will not betray friends."

"I won't ask you to. My heart's out of this."

"Where are you taking me?"

"We're headed for Texas, but I don't know if we'll make it that far."

"Do you think someone will catch us?" A gleam of hope sounded in Sarah's voice.

"You'd like that wouldn't you? Probably the Yanks will catch us, if they can." He looked toward the west, "We've got many miles to cover before we reach Texas."

"I don't have any desire to go to Texas."

"Where do you desire to go?" he asked.

"I haven't seen my father in several years. He was ill from his injuries. I'd like to go back up north and see him."

Adkisson was bitter. "You really sacrificed to get me. Was it worth it?"

"Yes, I think it was worth it. I saved some of our men— and I helped some slaves." She plucked at a blade of grass. "I wasn't able to stop the killing, but I think I've helped. I haven't bought your men to justice, but I think I've helped there too. In a way, I feel that I've avenged my father and his men."

"*Vengeance is mine, saith the Lord!*" he quoted.

"You're absolutely right there. I guess I deserved that. Just because I'm a Christian doesn't mean that I don't have lessons to learn too."

Adkisson eased his voice, "Don't some of the lessons grate?"

"They're not easy." Sarah looked away, "Like you said, it took years to *kind of* learn this one."

"What do you mean, *kind of*?" he asked.

"In your case, I've dealt with hatred for one enemy and one action, but that doesn't mean I would automatically apply it to anyone that hurt me and those I love. I have great resentment right now for what you did to Gideon."

"At least he's alive," he noted.

"I hope so, but I have no way of knowing that for sure."

"Believe me, I didn't hit him hard enough to kill him."

"Have you hit many people to come by this knowledge of how hard you must hit to kill a human being?" she asked.

"You are a trying woman. You could get on my nerves and make me want to hurt you."

"I'm not trying to be wearing, but I am trying to resurrect your conscience," she said.

"Umh!" he shook his head. "I can promise you this, if you behave yourself and don't give me trouble, I won't hurt you."

"What do you mean by *give you trouble*?" she asked.

"Get in my way, reveal me to the enemy— "

"*Big concession!* You know I have already done all of those. I will still bring you to justice, if I can."

"You don't care very much for your own life, do you?" he growled.

"Yes, I do want to live, but *some things* are worth dying for."

"I wouldn't die for the Confederacy." He turned away with nothing more to say.

Sarah dozed from their hard ride the past night. At dusk, she awakened to find Adkisson staring at her.

"Sorry, but I still can't believe you're in your early twenties."

"Yes, I've always had the problem of people thinking I was younger than I really am. I guess part of it is my size. Hard to be impressive when I'm so little."

"No, I think you underestimate yourself," he stated.

"How do you mean?"

"*You are impressive* and I can't imagine how I missed it before," he stated.

"I tried to be unimpressive. I needed to fade into the household and have others forget I was there."

"The more I get to know you, the more I realize, you were very strong. I always thought it a bit odd that you acted so responsibly when dealing with the slaves and the household. I explained it to myself that orphans need to grow up too fast."

"Some of the servants in the house were not slaves," she said.

"Why did they act like slaves then?" he asked.

"That was another part of our disguise"

"It doesn't really matter. They got their work done, don't guess they ever hurt me any," he said.

"No, they were good people," she paused. "You never fully appreciated any of them, or their work."

"What was I supposed to do, thank them every time they did their job?" he burst out angrily.

"It wouldn't have hurt and, it would have made them feel better."

"I'm not accustomed to thanking slaves when they do their job!"

"I didn't think you were, but that still doesn't make it right," she added.

"You're trying my patience again and one of *these times, you are going too far,*" Adkisson bit off.

"It doesn't really make any difference," she said.

"I can *make it* make a difference. You've had it easy so far, I can make it most unpleasant for you."

"I can imagine, but where God and one are gathered, they are the majority," she said.

"I wish you'd stop spouting that stuff. I can do to you what I want and you're not big enough to keep me from it."

"No, but in the long-run, I can't be beaten. I *will be victorious* through Jesus Christ."

"Even if I choose to kill you?" he asked.

"Even if you kill my body."

Adkisson rose and stalked away.

Sarah resumed her communion with God. *Oh, Lord, forgive us, when we trespass against others, forgive Montgomery Adkisson when he transgresses. . . Give me the words to say and the actions to back Your words. Give me peace, patience, forgiveness. . .*

Be with those left behind in New Orleans: Gideon, Clem, Cleota, Samuel, the household members. . . Keep them safe and bring them out of the paths of their enemies. Please end this war and bring peace to the nation; end this bondage of one human to another; bring all people to You in peace—consideration for one another.

Be with me, keep me in Your will. I praise You for the safety and peace You have given me already; patience for that to come.

"We've got to be on our way," he spoke softly, touched by this little woman, having observed her closed eyes and fervency.

As they rode through the night, Adkisson asked a question that had been bothering him. "You said you had forgiven me for your father and your fiancée, but you were working on it for Gideon?"

"Yes, I had time to deal with the first forgiveness, but the other I haven't dealt with. He was only a child. I can't understand you hitting a child."

"Why is your killing me right, and a blow to Gideon, not?" he asked.

"I am not accepting any killing, or injury to another! I am not killing you."

"I thought that was what you said?" he prompted.

"No, and I'm not forgiving your actions. I am able to forgive you as a person, but you make it harder when you continue to act in this brutal way toward others. If you were genuinely sorry for your acts of violence against others, then I think you would try not to do the same things again."

"Forgive the sinner and not the sin?" he asked.

"That's right. I think you had a little Bible teaching somewhere in your younger days. You need to remember it and act accordingly."

"That's harsh of you," he said.

"I'm not saying it's easy, but God can take away your sins, our sins. He won't even remember them any more if you are genuinely sorry for them and ask His forgiveness."

Sarah continued, "He doesn't say that humans are as good as He is. We probably will remember the bad you've done. We may even punish you for it someday," she added.

"I don't look forward to your kind of justice," he stated.

"No, but you have to face the consequences for your actions, even if God forgives you for them," she said.

"What does that do for you if you still have to face the consequences?" he asked.

"Let me tell you a story. Suppose a person is physically injured by his sin, he will always wear the scar, or the limp, or whatever the consequences are."

"I still don't quite see how that works," he said.

"Let me tell you a story from the Bible then."

"Not another Bible lesson!" he answered in a sullen manner. "I guess I can't get away from your voice?"

"If you let me go-"

"Not likely!" he muttered.

Quietly Sarah began. "There once was a very rich king that owned many flocks, but his neighbor had one little ewe lamb. The poor neighbor kept the little lamb inside his tent. He loved her like a little daughter. One day, the king had royal visitors and needed to prepare a feast for his guests. He sent out his servant to take the little lamb from his neighbor. They prepared the lamb and feasted. The neighbor family was broken hearted when they found their *daughter* lamb devoured."

He injected, "They should have been. I had a pet dog once our neighbors killed. We made him pay for it and the constable told him if he ever bothered our animals again, he'd have to pay the consequences."

"This story was told to King David by the prophet, Nathan." Sarah continued, "When King David was very angry at the rich man, Nathan said, *The rich king is you.*"

Sarah continued, "When King David came to realization of his sin, he fell on the floor and cried for mercy. He knew that Nathan was speaking to him about what he had done."

"What did he do?" Adkisson asked.

"Even though King David had many wives, he took the only wife of one of his faithful soldiers away from her husband and then had the man killed. The firstborn son, born to King David and Bathsheba, died. There was continual family strife all the rest of David's life. The family problems were the consequences of David's flaunting of God's laws. His family was never able to get along with each other. If a father doesn't set a good example for his children, they may follow in his footsteps and cause him and everyone else problems for years."

She continued, "David's children continued to cheat and war against each other until many of them died or were killed. Most of them did not fulfill their role or potential because of the father's poor example."

Adkisson's interest had been prodded. He listened intently. "Yes, I guess I've seen consequences played out in some people I've known."

"Your men wounded my father, hurt my uncle and killed my fiancée. They still bear the consequences of your actions. You still bear the scars too."

Adkisson was in thought for a moment, "Why did God punish your family, they weren't the ones in the wrong?" he asked.

"No, but God doesn't always stand in the way of evil when it comes along. My family got in the way of your hirelings. Good people bear the consequences too, sometimes from the actions of those who do evil.""

"That's not a very *just* God," he stated bitterly.

"No, but in the long run, the godly people will have a reward."

"But the evil may get a reward too," he said.

"They might get a temporary benefit, but that won't last. Sometime they will pay for what they've done."

"When will I have to pay?" he asked.

"That's not for me to say, but ultimately God will be the judge, even if the punishment has to wait until after the death of the person who committed the deed."

"Oh, now you're getting to heaven and hell," he said.

"That's right. Those who believe in Jesus Christ, accept His forgiveness, and ask Him to save them will go to heaven."

"And?" he asked.

"And those who don't, go to hell to burn for eternity."

"How can a loving God put someone in hell?" Adkisson asked the classic question of unbelievers,

"God doesn't," Sarah answered.

"A person wouldn't put himself in hell, if he had a choice," he stated emphatically.

"Oh, but he does. If he doesn't choose God, he has made the decision against God and he sends himself to hell," she stated.

"That's a hard one," he said.

"Yes, it is hard to know God's mind, because we are so far below Him. He is merciful and He does love us. He's just waiting for us to come to Him. He never leaves us."

"You mean he's here now?" he asked.

"Yes, I've felt His presence, haven't you?" she added.

Montgomery shivered. "No, I haven't seen him. If I choose to kill you, I don't think he'd stop me."

"He might not, but I'd be fine, alive or dead," she said.

"How could that be? You'd just be dead."

"But I'd be with Him in heaven if I was dead, or I'm still alive here on earth and He will still be with me. I'm the winner, no matter what happens to me."

"That's beyond me."

"I'm praying for you. If you want, it won't have to be beyond your understanding," Sarah said softly.

Adkisson shook his head, "*Not now!* I've got to get us to Texas. I don't want to think about it."

"You can't stop me from praying as long as I'm alive. I hope you will think about it. What better time than when someone is chasing you? You need someone to help you *now*!"

"Be quiet, Sarah."

They rode in silence, but sometimes Sarah whispered prayers aloud. Montgomery Adkisson didn't stop her.

❧

After a silent hour, he said, "I admire your courage in adverse situations."

"It's not mine, it's the Lord's," Sarah said.

"Always a sermon! I'm glad I didn't see this part of your character while you worked for me." He rubbed the trickle of sweat from between his eyes. "I'll take that statement back, while you worked *against me*."

Four Days Out of New Orleans in the Bayous

Sarah tried again to reason with Montgomery Adkisson, "The soldiers are overflowing this region, they'll be sure to catch us. Turn me loose. You can travel much faster alone."

He paused, "Where would you go?"

"I could walk to a house when we cross a road or down the Red River."

"What if they catch on that you're a Yankee?"

"You didn't."

"It might be rather dangerous to be here alone."

She looked at him, "And it *isn't dangerous being kidnaped* and carried off toward Texas by a Confederate in possibly his enemy's territory?"

He grinned, "Touché."

They rested the latter part of the day. Sarah drifted and awakened several times before a full moon showed Adkisson staring at the dying coals of their meager fire.

She rolled and offered her back to the scene; heard him shifting several times and finally his regular breathing as he slept.

I could get away. He's bound to be tired, we've ridden hard; he hasn't rested well for four days? She stretched one leg from under the cloth she used to ward off the bite of insects. *No sound*, she paused, then shifted her other leg and raised onto her elbow. She pulled one knee under her and braced her other leg to crawl to her knees. She gathered her skirt and bunched it in her hand, so she could move without stepping on her full skirt. Tension filled her body.

A gruff voice sounded, "Where are you going?"

She turned slowly. "I didn't want to waken you, but I need to go to the bushes."

"All right, but don't take too long, or I'll be after you."

I must appear to make good my request.

She walked into the underbrush, took a long breath and steadied her shaking limbs. She flexed her fingers and shook her arms several times to relieve tension. After a few moments, she parted the brush and looked back to see him sitting in the moonlight with his face toward his feet. As she hesitated, his head turned, he looked directly at the place where she had vanished into the trees.

I've got to go back, no matter how much I'd like to run. I can't get far enough away on foot now. I will need a better place to make a run. If the horse totally gives out, I'd have a better chance of hiding and outrunning him.

When she walked back toward their campsite, he raised his face to her, but didn't stand.

"Please sit down, I have something to discuss with you," he stated.

She gathered her full skirt and seated herself on her ground cover. She couldn't see his expression and was glad that he probably, couldn't see hers. *I feel so guilty and I've done nothing wrong. Dear God, help me deal with this man. Bring him around, change him.*

"What was it you wanted?" she asked.

"I've been thinking, we could make a good life together. Like I told you, we'll get to Texas and start over there. We'd marry and neither of us will bring up the other's background. We'll begin brand new."

She looked down to hide her shock and remained quiet for a moment.

He spoke quietly, "Don't you have anything to say to my proposal?"

She refused to consider the proposal, "What if Texas falls to the Yankees, what do you intend to do then?"

"We could go to Mexico, or South America. I hear there's southerners there already."

"You forget several things," she said.

"What?"

"First, I'm not in love with you and have no intention of ever marrying you. I've never done anything to make you think otherwise."

"No, you've been exemplary." He hesitated a moment, " May I ask, what is the second reason?"

"I'm northern through and through, southern life is beyond me."

"You don't think you could come to enjoy the good life with me?" he asked.

"No."

"You wouldn't consider my offer?"

"There are other reasons, of which I've never spoken to you," she said.

"What?"

"I could not link myself in marriage to someone who isn't devoted first to Jesus Christ." Her voice carried an obvious sadness.

The pair was silent for a time.

He spoke first, "How long have you looked for those who attempted the robbery at your father's iron works?"

"Thirty-one months and fourteen days."

"Why so precise in your calculations of the time?" he asked.

"If the dearest people you love are killed or injured by others, don't you think you'd remember?"

"Hah, where's the Christianity you've been telling me so much about?" he growled.

"Like you said, God says *vengeance is mine*, but He

doesn't say that we can't help the law along," she stated.

"The law of the north, is not my law. You must remember, I owe no allegiance to your Union."

"If the north is victorious, this region will come under their command *and you will be* within the power of their law."

"It amazes me, I have underestimated you, Sarah."

"We probably make that mistake with many people we meet," Sarah said.

Adkisson smirked, "You might think about God's forgiveness, of which you are so ready to tell me."

She looked down. *Lord, sometimes I am unforgiving.*

"Sarah— ," he hesitated, "get some sleep. We need to be away early and that time is drawing near."

They arose at one AM. After a meager feed, he helped her up behind the saddle.

Two hours later, the horse stumbled through the mud of a bayou.

"You've got to release me, this creature can't stand up to this load much longer. If you want to get away, you'll have to go on alone."

"Well, you continue to be honest with me about your feelings, but I can't turn you loose. Right now, you are my only protection. When I get out of this area . . . I don't know." He slid down off the horse and led it ahead, with Sarah still aboard.

"I can walk too. This poor horse is worn out."

"No!" He looked up to see her flinch from his harshly spoken word. He softened, "Whether you like the southerners or not, they are a courteous people. I won't have a woman walking unless things get much worse than they are now."

Sarah couldn't let it rest. "Why do southerners require their slave women to walk behind the master's conveyance if they are so courteous to women?"

"I don't consider them women."

"Oh, but they are. Cleota has been my dearest friend since I was a babe. If it hadn't been for her, I probably wouldn't be alive now."

"Who's Cleota?" he asked.

"The woman you sent away."

"That slave woman? I can't even remember, what was that all about?"

"She was defending me, as she always has."

"It wasn't her place," he stated flatly.

"Why not? I've been like her own child all my life. Maternal instinct is very strong."

"I won't discuss slaves with you." His voice was flat.

"She was never a slave in New Orleans."

He turned quickly to look into her face. "What do you mean, she wasn't a slave? She was in the house I leased and the slaves were part of the bargain."

"Remember? I told you before, that was what we wanted you to think, but she was never a slave in that house."

"Why did she work there then?" he asked.

"She was with me." A warning sounded in Sarah's mind, *Don't name names, you still may endanger the others.*

He raised his hand. "It's over and done with, she's gone to the back country. We're not in the house now. I don't want to hear anymore about her, or any of the other *servants*, as you call them."

"That's fine with me," Sarah said.

"We're too tired to be formal, call me Montgomery and I'm going to call you Sarah."

Sarah was too tired to object.

Montgomery plodded on in silence leading the tired animal. Sarah rocked along and dozed in the saddle. Suddenly, she was slammed awake by the harsh grip of hands at her waist and jerked upright against the hard chest of her captor.

"Are you hurt? You must have fallen asleep, I caught you just in time to prevent you hitting the ground.!"

"Thank— you. I guess I did go to sleep. Sorry I didn't stay more alert."

"Are you awake now?"

"Yes, you can let me go now," she said.

"If you'd marry me, I would take care of you all the time." He dropped his head and drew her closer.

She was afraid he meant to kiss her. She spoke quietly, "No, I still can't marry you."

He jerked his arms away from her. "Then take care of yourself!"

Sarah staggered. "I am grateful you kept me from falling, but if you'd let me leave, then you wouldn't have to worry about me any longer."

He sounded irritable and desperate, "Will you quit asking me to let you go? I've already said that I can't."

"Think about it, you'll see that it makes sense," she said.

He swung aboard the horse, "Are you going to walk or get back on this horse?"

"I would prefer to walk, if I may?"

"I shouldn't have asked. I can't let you walk while I ride. Put your foot in the stirrup and give me your hand." He swung her up behind him again and she arranged her skirts.

"Are you settled, Miss Hen?" Amusement sounded in his voice.

"Why did you call me that?"

"You reminded me of a little hen with ruffled feathers that I once knew" he said.

"I didn't know that you ever noticed *animals*?"

"Yes, I do notice, especially good horses and good women."

"Women are hardly animals."

"They've got a lot of the same characteristics. Like those ruffled feathers when they're disturbed."

She had to laugh.

"Do you find that amusing?"

"No, it's just good to find that you're a little human in some ways."

They trudged on in silence.

The day heated. They rode under the shade of a huge live oak tree and dismounted under its concealing branches.

"We'll rest here until it gets cooler. There's a little stream fifty feet away, I'll take the horse for water and tie him off to graze. You can come to the stream and freshen up in a few minutes."

She leaned against the tree, sank down exhausted, then slept.

A half hour later, he came back and settled himself in the shade. He propped his head on the saddle and before he dozed off, watched her for a few moments.

He spoke under his breath, "Beautiful and bedraggled, don't know why I never noticed it. If she'd only come around, I know we could be happy."

After two hours, he touched her shoulder to awaken her, "We must be on our way. Go to the stream now, we may not have another chance for a while."

Hostage

Samuel and Clem were terrified as they searched for Sarah, first in the house, then for Gideon to ask of her. Neither were to be found.

"Strange. Gideon never leaves the place, unless Sarah sends him somewhere and now they're both gone!" Clem stated.

"I'm afraid that something bad has happened to her. Let's see if anyone else in the house knows where Sarah is," Samuel replied.

"She went to the verandah with young Massa," was the only answer they received from the servants.

After a frantic search of the gardens and the carriage house, they still turned up no evidence of her.

"I'll check the office again. You go see if Gideon has returned," Samuel ran his hand through his disheveled hair. As he passed through the office, a scrap of paper lay on the floor in front of the overturned desk chair. He picked it up, smoothed it flat on the desk.

The scrawl read, *They are on to us. Get out quick. Take the girl as a shield, she's a SPY. L. A.*

Clem burst into the house. "He took Sarah with him!"

"Who?" Samuel looked shocked.

"Adkisson! I found Gideon in back of the house. His head was bleeding but he was sitting up talking to himself. He told me that Adkisson took Sarah and knocked him down when he tried to stop the man," Clem said.

"No! please don't let him hurt Sarah," Samuel pleaded.

"The boy said the master hit her on the arm, but she was able to walk to the stables. Gideon wasn't able to help her and he's still having trouble standing up. I carried him to the servants at his house and came straight over here," Clem shook his head.

"I found this note in the study. I think it has some bearing on what you just said." Samuel held out the wrinkled scrap.

Clem looked at the note. "I think you're right. Let's go check the stables. Maybe we can find out what they took and ask the servants which way they went."

"Fine." The two ran out through the gardens of the house where Sarah had lived the past years.

They found no horses standing in the stalls.

"You suppose Adkisson took a horse, or have the soldiers already been here?" Clem asked.

"How can we know?" Samuel asked.

"I think I'd better go talk to Gideon again, maybe he has regained enough strength so that he can remember," Clem turned to go.

"The saddles and bridles are gone too, nothing left but harness and old leather goods. When they left, they must have ridden, or walked away." Sam made a discouraging remark, "I pray Gideon can remember."

"There's fresh droppings here, I'd say he still had his horse in this stall," Clem said.

The two moved quickly around the fence and approached the back door of the neighboring home.

"We need to speak to Gideon," Samuel stated.

"He's in the kitchen," the washerwoman said. "Go through dis dor."

Clem and Samuel stepped on the verandah and into the

indicated door. Gideon lay on a narrow cot near the wall, but he turned his head and tried to sit up when he saw the two men.

"Stay down, Gideon. We have something we must ask you," Samuel said.

"Have you found Miss Sarah?" Gideon was anxious.

"No, I'm afraid not, but maybe you can help us," Clem said.

"Whut?"

"Did Adkisson have a horse in the stables?" Samuel asked.

"Yes, suh."

"Did they ride away when he left with Miss Sarah?" Clem asked.

"Yes'um and they turned right out of the carriage house and down the road," Gideon said.

"That was my next question. Do you have any idea where they went?" Samuel asked.

"No." Gideon turned his eyes down, tears dripped from his face, but he made no sound. It was easy to see he felt he had let his best friend down.

Samuel patted the boy's shoulder, he wanted to relay hope. "We're going to find them. You can help by telling us exactly what that horse looks like."

Gideon wiped the side of his face and looked up. His face fairly shone. "Massa's horse was a sorrel with a white snip, he had three white feet, the right hind was solid color and he was a gelding."

"Was he a big horse, or of any certain kind?"

"He was fancy, had a high head. He wouldn't nevah stand still. Massa said he was a saddle horse and better'n most."

"Was he shod all around?" Samuel asked.

"Yes suh and he was big. Miss Sarah couldn't get on him by herself, Massa had to help her on."

"Did they take any food?" Clem asked.

"He had a tow sack of some'in in front of da saddle."

"Thanks Gideon, I think that's all we need to know. Was there anything else you think we ought to know?" Clem asked.

"No, suh. Can you find her?"

"We're going to try," Samuel replied.

"We need to go now, but I'm sure we'll be back. Get well Gideon." Clem put his hand on the side of the boy's head that was not injured.

"Yes. It will make Miss Sarah very happy to know that you are fine again," Samuel added.

Clem turned to the washerwoman on the porch. He withdrew coins from his pocket and placed them in her hand. "See that he gets proper care. When we return, I'll give you more."

"He ain't mine," she replied.

"We know. You like money of your own don't you?"

"Yes, Suh."

"Then you don't have to say anything about it, just take extra care of him."

"Yes, um. I shore will."

The two left Gideon on his cot in his master's kitchen.

On the way to the stables, Samuel spoke to Clem, "With the troops in town, I'm sure we're free to finish this job."

"Let's look at the tracks out of the carriage house. The horse may have something different that will help us follow him," Clem directed.

"Yes, I have a feeling we're going to be trailing that animal for several days and I'd like to be sure we're following the right one," Samuel replied.

They examined the soft earth near the gate in the wrought iron fence.

"Fresh shod, the cogs are very distinct, just as Gideon

said," Samuel said.

"He drags that left front foot a little when he sits it down." Clem pointed at a drag mark in the soft dirt of the roadside.

"But when he gets lined out, he may not," Samuel added.

"Yes, the horse is only walking here and he's not warmed up. Adkisson didn't want to draw attention to himself and his captive by racing away."

"The horse may get better when he's traveled a bit. Now, let's go to headquarters and see if we can get horses and supplies to catch them," Samuel said.

"Good idea. We won't need anything they can't give us. Let's go right now, so the trail won't get any colder."

"We can ask at headquarters if any one knows if a man and woman left town on one horse," Samuel said.

"There were probably many leaving, but it won't hurt to ask," Clem said.

The two hurried to the military Governor's headquarters. When his aide furnished the two with three horses, passes, weapons, and provisions, they rode to the west edge of New Orleans with the blessings of the commanding general's occupying troops.

"I think he'd have to go west as soon as he got around the marshes near the city," Samuel said.

"Yes, if he went to far north, he'd be in trouble," Clem replied.

"Unless they got a boat, they couldn't go far south, east wouldn't be too smart. The river is up, that don't leave many routes out of the city." Samuel fidgeted while he attempted to make a decision.

"I've prayed and I am in agreement with you, we should circle around the edge of the city on the northwest. See if we can find anyone who saw them pass, or pick up any kind of a trail," Clem suggested.

"We're only a few hours behind them. Riding double, they won't be able to get too far ahead of us— unless he had more horses stashed somewhere. His horse is probably not in as good condition as this trio. He's been in New Orleans for months and the feedstuffs haven't been easily available for some time," Samuel added.

"Oh, God. Please let that be the case. Make his horse so out of condition he can't run fast or far!" lamented Clem.

"Let's split up, you check a mile this way and I'll check a mile that way. Ask everyone you see. We'll meet back here in about an hour."

"Fine, be careful with your horses, there are people still trying to get out of the city and they may rob us if they get the chance," Clem directed.

The two went their own ways; Samuel led the extra mount behind his horse.

Each road heading from the north and west sides of New Orleans were carefully checked by the two men. Refugees flowed out of the city in any conveyance they could find. When asked if they had seen a man and a woman on one horse, several indicated they had. When further details were sought, each gave the wrong description of the horse, or riders.

Clem returned to the starting point. Samuel was nowhere to be seen.

Please, let Sam find someone who saw them leave town, Clem prayed as he waited.

"Over here, Clem."

The two converged on the main road out of town.

"I didn't find anyone who gave a good description of people like Sarah and Adkisson," Clem said in frustration.

"I don't think he'd take this road, it has too many on it," Samuel replied.

"Let's ride northwest and see if we can strike his trail."

"I've been thinking that too. I think they might have gone upriver headed north and then they'll turn west. The terrain up there would be better for cross-country riding," Samuel guessed.

"Yes, there are too many swamps here. You'd never be able to get a horse through unless you stayed on some kind of road."

"I don't think he'll stay on the main roads until he gets out further away from town."

"Say your prayers. If we've made a mistake—" Clem didn't want to finish the thought.

"Let's move!"

Clem and Samuel rode at a steady pace. They stopped twice to water the horses and that evening they grained the trio. The two men ate cold beans, reluctant to build a fire and risk bringing in deserters or someone needing a horse.

The next day, they hung to the road during the daytime, passed other refugees, but never found evidence of Sarah or her captor.

Doubt crept in.

"I think we should cast south now in hopes of crossing their trail," Samuel thought aloud.

"We might be ahead of them by now." Clem wiped his face with his handkerchief. "Sure is hot in here, hope Sarah's doing all right."

"It's not an easy ride. Let's go out one more day, before we turn south," Samuel said.

"What if they went up the Red River?" Clem speculated.

"That's a possibility, but it would be further north yet."

"We could split up, but I don't think that's a good idea," Clem said.

"No, I'm sure that Adkisson will be armed and we may need more than one to keep him from hurting Sarah."

"We may run into Rebs too."

"That's a distinct possibility."

"We've lost a lot of time and found nothing."

The pair turned slightly south.

Near dusk, when they cast up and down the banks of a muddy creek for a crossing, they spied tracks at the edge of the water.

"Look, there are the tracks of a man here beside the horse. He looks to have gotten a drink," Clem pointed a finger.

"Look here!" Samuel spoke in a hushed voice.

"Small tracks, a woman, or a child. Do you think they could be Sarah's?" Clem asked.

"I'm afraid to hope, but I think so."

"They're not far ahead of us. We'll have to go quietly, but I think we should try to follow these tracks."

"This is the best lead we've had so far. Maybe we'll be able to tell before long."

The trailing pair waited for their horses to drink, then they remounted and crossed the creek.

"The tracks lead out of the stream at a diagonal, let's · follow," Samuel said.

"We're fairly close. I think one of us should follow directly on the tracks and the other should take the pack horse and stay off to one side," Clem reasoned.

"We'd better use hand signals. Don't want someone hearing us and laying an ambush," Samuel guessed.

Clem thought aloud, "I'm the best tracker, I'll stay on the trail."

"We can trade off, if you want?"

"That's fine, let's move on." Clem moved his hand on the reins and pressed his heels to his horse's belly.

After two hours, Clem signaled Samuel closer to him. They stopped behind a screen of trees.

"It's getting dark, I can't see the tracks. I'm afraid if we go further, we'll lose 'em," Clem whispered.

"Let's make a dry camp right here and both of us circle out on foot— maybe a couple of miles. See if we can see a camp ahead," Samuel said.

"Gotta be quiet, don't want to stampede them."

"Looks to me like they been traveling some at night. That may help keep them out of the way of marauders. Adkisson may think it will make them harder to follow."

"They may not be in the same spot by morning, but I'd rather come up on them during the day," Clem remarked.

"I can see where the horse browsed at times. He stood mostly in the same spot, wasn't tied out with enough rope to find much to eat," Samuel pointed to a trampled place in the ground.

"He'll be giving out. I see Adkisson's tracks more and more."

"You don't see the smaller tracks?"

"No, I think he's letting the smaller rider stay aboard," Clem remarked.

"Okay, let's settle in and get moving before it gets any later. The moon will soon be up, that'll help us find our way back to this camp," Samuel said.

"Yes, there's a fork in the creek here, if we need a land mark, that ought to help. These bushes hide the animals well."

"No great need for them to graze, they've still got oats."

"The nose bags will keep them quieter than anything we could do for them," Clem stated.

Their animals stationed, the two walked away in opposite directions to make their forward quarter circles.

One hour later, Samuel limped back into camp. Clem wasn't long showing up.

"Nothing!" Clem snorted softly.

"Nothing on my side either and I managed to twist my ankle under a root."

"Is it bad?"

"No, just a nuisance." Samuel carefully removed his boot and stuck his foot into the creek.

"Guess we better get some sleep, if that's possible with these mosquitoes."

"Yeah, we'll have to be up at dawn to continue our search," Samuel agreed.

Wish I Knew How to Pray

Exhausted, Adkisson loaded the horse. The fleeing couple found themselves stumbling along.

Tonight, Sarah refused to mount the weary horse. "It's cruel, he's more exhausted than we are. We've got to find him some grain or he's going to be lost. I can't stand to see him suffer anymore."

"He's coming along. We'll go up along the Red at daylight and find some grain."

"If we can't, I think we ought to turn him loose and let him find his own forage. We should have thought of a rope, then he could graze during the day."

Adkisson was losing his patience with this talkative little woman, "On what?"

"There's all kinds of undergrowth, that would be better than nothing."

"When we reach the river, we'll look for a rope or something to stake him out. That's the best I can do for now."

"We could lay over for a couple of days and let him recover."

"I'm not about to. Someone may be following us. I'll take to the river rather than lay around here and waste time."

"You don't really think anyone was able to follow us from New Orleans?" Sarah's hopes rose, than sank.

Exhaustion wore them down, but she still hoped to

lower his vigilance and escape, or cause him to leave her behind. Occasionally she made a scuff mark or broke a twig as they rode along.

"No one would have been able to follow us on the roads where there were so many tracks." She thought a moment. *We cut cross-country. I used to hear people say that Indians could track anywhere.* "Outside of a miracle, I don't see anyone coming."

"I thought you were praying for a miracle?" he said.

"I have been."

"You have been? What about now, have you lost faith in your God?"

"I still am praying. I haven't lost my faith in God and you better get some faith, because if you don't, we're going to die out here walking through this dismal swamp! We may die of malaria from these mosquito bites," she flipped her hand where mosquitoes buzzed in anticipation of a warm meal.

"I didn't bring along any medicine," he said.

"No, we left too quickly to think of some of the things we might need."

"What else did we forget?" he asked.

"A rope for the horse, and I could certainly use some clean clothes."

"Why, Madam, you look devastating in your shredded skirt!"

"If we'd lay-over a day, I could wash out some of our things. That would at least make us feel better. I'd love to sink into a tub and soak for days. My feet are so tired."

"That would be good."

"Do they have bath houses along the river?" she asked.

"I'm sure they do at the larger cities," Adkisson said.

"My father and I never went up the Red. What cities are there?" Sarah intended to learn all she could about their location.

Near first light, they reached a possible camp site. Sarah stepped behind bushes and removed her petticoats. The waistband made one strong cord, but it wasn't long enough. She ripped the cloth into strips from top to bottom of the skirt, tied several together, then rolled the long strands.

"This may do, or I could braid the strips. I never hobbled a horse, so I don't know which would be best. What do you think?" she asked.

"I think it's soft and will work. I'll put this rolled one on. Braid a couple more and we'll see if we can make a longer lead. If he won't tolerate these hobbles, maybe we could stake him out with a longer length."

Sarah scooted down beside a large tree and began to braid.

When Adkisson came back, she was asleep over her work. He looked at her and made up his mind not to disturb her, unless the horse caused trouble.

He muttered to himself. *The horse has his head down, he's too exhausted to graze. I watered him. I hope he revives today, or I may have to turn him loose. Wish I'd thought about a little grain for him, or finding an extra horse. It's been too much for him.* He rested his head on Sarah's tree. "Wish I knew how to pray, I'd ask for a miracle."

"Humh? What did you say? I must have dozed off." She resumed her braiding.

"I said, I wish I knew how to pray, I'd ask for a miracle."

"You can pray, all you have to do is talk to God, but you have to believe, or He won't hear your prayer."

"What good will it do to pray, if he doesn't hear?"

"He does hear the sinner's prayer."

"What's that?" he asked.

"That's where you admit you've done the wrong things, ask Him to forgive you and tell Him that you believe in Him.

Then start praying," she explained.

"That simple?"

"It really is. Confess, believe and ask, couldn't be much easier than that."

"Maybe for you. If I had it to do over, I'd still probably do the same thing again. I wouldn't try to rob the Turner Iron Works. Now, I know that didn't work and I'm sorry that I hurt your father and uncle."

"What about Daniel and Gideon?"

"I'm not so sure on those two."

"Why?" she asked.

"If Daniel were alive, you wouldn't be here with me."

His words turned her heart to stone. "That's probably true, but I'll try to ignore your thoughts on Daniel." She was silent while she sought to move away from her thoughts of Daniel's death. "What about Gideon?"

"He got in my way."

"Haven't I gotten in your way too?" she asked.

"I guess, but somehow that's different."

"Not really, either one of us would still stop you, if we could."

"Keep still. Sarah, sometimes you talk too much."

"That's the way with women, I guess. *They talk and men act*, that's the nature of the creatures. I can tell you one thing though."

"What's that?" he asked.

"If women were running this war, we'd have already talked it out, *and* we wouldn't have shot at each other."

"I will have to admit, that might be true," he agreed.

"I'm finished with this petticoat rope."

"Lay it there and get some sleep. I'm too tired to put it on him now and he isn't going anywhere."

At dusk, Adkisson roused himself and looked at the horse picking at the shrubs around him. "Well, guess he got a little forage under his cinch. I'll water him again and try to fill him up that way."

He touched Sarah's shoulder, "Rise and shine, time to go find this animal something more substantial."

"Leave me here and I'll come along later," she said wearily.

"No, we've got to stay together. You'd be lost alone and I still need you."

"I can't get my shoes on, my feet are too swollen."

"Here, soak your feet a minute, then you'll be able to get your shoes back on. I'll fix a little coffee while you sit here."

"Maybe the water and the coffee will wake me up."

❦

Following the fugitive and Sarah, Clem and Sam were ready to call it a day. Night was descending again.

"Do you smell smoke?" Clem asked.

"No, but I think I smell coffee."

The pair savored the breeze coming from the northwest.

"It may be our imagination," Clem said.

"We'd better go check," Samuel said.

"We can't take the horses, one of them would nicker. They'd give us away for sure," Clem whispered.

"We've only got two pairs of hands to hold three noses. We could take the two we're riding, but this one would be sure to raise a ruckus if left here alone. Anybody within two miles would be sure to hear him."

"I think we'd better tie the horses here and check ahead on foot. If it's deserters or refugees, we may need to slip up on them," Clem added.

"We need to find out how many there are, there could be a whole army in these woods. Tie the animals and let's put on their feed bags," Samuel replied.

"That'll keep them happy until we return," Clem whispered.

"We need to spread out about twenty yards apart and keep low until we get close. Then we may have to crawl."

"Keep an eye peeled, if we see anything, draw back and we'll decide the next move."

"Let's go. I think I can follow my nose to that fire."

Not a sound came from the two, as they stealthily moved forward. Within four hundred yards from their horses, they heard a voice. Both dropped to their stomachs and crept forward. The undergrowth was thick. They couldn't see far.

Samuel's path was full of thorny vines; he squirmed forward on his belly. Rabbit runs were profuse under the vines. He angled into one.

The voices grew louder. He overheard the sweet tones of a woman. She spoke a mild protest.

"You must go on alone and find some grain for the horse. My feet are still swollen. Leave me the coffee and some of those hard crackers," she said.

"No, I'm not leaving you. We don't have far. The horse can carry you today."

"But he's too worn out," she pleaded.

"I'll put you on. You can tie your shoes to the saddle. Maybe having your feet exposed this morning will give you some relief."

"I can't even hobble over there," the female voice said.

"I'll bring him to you. Stay there."

Clem and Samuel could see Sarah. They could hear Adkisson speaking to the horse while saddling the animal.

Samuel had all he could do to restrain himself. If he could get up out of the brambles, he could reach Sarah before Adkisson got back, but that was not what he and Clem had planned. He lay still, watched the proceedings in the clearing. His chance slipped away in seconds.

Adkisson came back and heaved Sarah aboard the big horse. The animal had regained a reprieve from his exhaustion and followed the man away. The three turned to the northwest and moved off.

When the man and his hostage were out of sight, Clem spoke to Samuel, "Psst, are you there?"

"Yeah, but I had a terrible time keeping from grabbing Sarah."

"Me too, if we'd planned it before, I was closer to him, and you to Sarah. I could have gotten him, while you grabbed her," Clem said.

"Now we know where they're headed, let's try to keep up. If the opportunity arises, grab the one closest to you, and I'll take the other," Samuel directed.

They followed the plodding pair for hours.

Samuel spoke first, "These roads are closer together."

"I figure we're nearing some kind of a town or crossroad," Clem commented.

"We'd better hang back, this is southern territory and I don't want to bust in on a local militia, armed and ready," Samuel said.

"Me neither. I don't think they'll stay long, we can catch up as they leave."

"They're starting to travel later in the morning."

"I'd like to catch them before dark," Clem stated.

"If that don't work, after they go to sleep."

"I wonder if he lets her out of his sight?"

"Probably not far, she's still trying to persuade him to let her go," Samuel said.

"Keep the horses below the hill. One of us better shinny up there and peep over before we breast that hill and expose ourselves," Clem directed.

"I'll go ahead." Samuel crawled to the brow of the hill and looked over. Before him lay a ferry landing on the river, a couple of hard scrabble houses, and a tavern. He saw

Adkisson and Sarah approach the tavern.

He turned back down the hill to Clem.

"They're going into the inn. They'll probably eat, maybe rest a bit, they might even take time to clean up."

"Do you think he'd let her out of his sight long enough for all that?" Clem asked.

"I don't know, but he's southern and might be able to convince these people that she came willingly," Samuel answered.

"Could he scare her enough to make her keep quiet?"

"I'm not sure. I didn't see any women around. I think they would come nearer helping her than the men would."

"Yes, unless the men's southern hospitality thought they were rescuing a damsel in distress," Clem put in.

"A Yankee spy? Hardly," Samuel grinned.

"He'd be afraid to tell them that, they'd lynch her right on the spot," Clem said.

"They could, but that might be how he'd convince her she was safer with him. We'd best settle down here somewhere and wait them out. Let's not give her any more trouble," Samuel said.

"You know the lay of the land, I'll go back a ways and get the horses out of sight, then I'll come back to this spot and wait," Clem said.

"I'll find a good spot on the hill and keep an eye on the doings down there. If I see them leaving, I'll whistle like a mocking bird, then you can bring the horses here, but keep them out of sight."

"Will do. See you later." Clem turned away.

"Keep safe and keep praying for us all."

"I will. Same to you."

The day was heavy with humidity. Samuel flexed his cramped muscles and rolled to his other side. He was having trouble keeping his eyes open. Once, he saw Adkisson come and get his tow sack from the saddle.

The horse stood in exhausted patience where he was tied to the hitching rail. The animal's head drooped, the dull hide on his gaunt sides looked like a rack of bare bones.

A boy came out and led the animal to a small shed out back, but no one else came from the inn. Samuel slipped back down the hill and spoke to Clem.

"Adkisson came out to the house for his tow sack. They took the horse to the shed. I'd say they're all being fed. There are two half-grown draft mules in the corral, but I don't think they'd want to ride those. I think they'll be awhile, but I'll go back up and keep my eyes open."

"I can go up, if you want to change off," Clem volunteered.

"Can you whistle like a mocking bird?" Samuel asked.

"I think I can make an out of it."

"Okay, I am thirsty, I'll drop back to the horses and then I'll come right back. I need to stretch my legs and get woke up."

The sun crept toward the west. Samuel wormed his way up beside Clem. He whispered, "Do you think they're going to spend the night?"

"Don't know. They may," Clem replied.

The two watched the inn.

"There comes that boy back out."

"Yes, and he's going out back." The pair watched.

"Here he comes back with Adkisson's horse."

"And Adkisson is coming out." They waited a few moments.

"Where's Sarah?" Clem asked.

Adkisson fiddled with his saddle strings and stowed the bulging tow sack back in front of the saddle.

"Looks like they got fresh supplies."

The man stepped back to the door and spoke to

someone inside.

A woman appeared. "That's Sarah, I'd recognize her anywhere. They've found some different clothes."

"Yeah, looks like they're ready to start. He's putting her up on the horse, but he's still on the ground."

"Guess, he's still going to lead the animal."

"They all look better," Clem said.

"They may be harder to manage now. Before they were worn out," Samuel commented.

"Get the horses. Let's go through the trees to that side of town," Clem directed.

By the time Adkisson lined out on his direction, night was advancing quickly. The two men followed behind at a distance that was out of sight and hearing.

"We've got to be careful, they may lay up soon and we don't want to come up on them unexpectedly."

"No, guess we'll have to stop and catch back up in the morning."

"I thought we almost had them, now we've got to creep up in the daytime. You think they'll sleep during the day, like they were doing?"

"Don't know, but we'll be ready. Bed down and we'll get an early start."

"We're half way across Louisiana, if we don't get them soon, we'll hit Texas."

"That may make it harder than ever," Samuel said.

"I think we'd better make a raid before much longer," Clem said.

"Yes, let's push closer today and try to hit them as soon as we get a chance," Samuel agreed.

"Do you still think surprise is the best?"

"I think we'd be less likely to have to use force."

"Adkisson isn't going to go without a fight. He's run too far for that!"

"We know he's armed. He's got a scabbard on the front

of his saddle. Sarah said he always carried a concealed derringer up his right sleeve," Clem reminded Samuel.

"Say, that reminds me, Sarah carried a derringer too. Wonder why she hasn't used it?" Samuel asked.

"Do you *really* think that Sarah would use a pistol on *anyone*," Clem asked?

"No, I expect you're right, drawing a pistol doesn't seem quite right for her. Wonder if she still has it? She might be convincing if she *acted* like she was going to use it," Samuel said.

"I don't know, I'd say she would have used it to protect Gideon, but I doubt she'd use it to protect herself. She probably didn't have time when Adkisson got her and hit Gideon," Clem said.

"Gideon said he crawled under the fence at a ground hog hole. I doubt that Sarah or Adkisson expected him to rise up out of the earth like that."

"You're probably right. I think that all happened very fast."

"If this goes on much longer, I'm going to lose my patience and make *something* happen fast," Samuel said.

"We've been patient this long, hang in there a little longer. I can feel the Lord moving to help us out," Clem said.

"I can see them getting tired again. They won't make much time today."

"Looks to me like they're bedded down already," Clem whispered.

"I think you're right. This traveling by daylight is easier than keeping them in sight at night."

"I've got a feeling that tonight's our night. Let's tie the horses here and go ahead on foot," Clem said.

"Go slow, give them time to settle in," Samuel said.

The two men lay together watching preparation for a night camp. They saw Adkisson feed the horse a small measure of grain, then he staked the animal out in a decent patch of grass.

They saw Sarah gather a few small twigs and some dry wood. She stacked it near a downed log.

Adkisson came back with the tow sack and lit the wood. He set the coffee pot on the log and laid out a loaf of bread. He appeared to be slicing bread, while the coals burned down.

Sarah sat next to a tree and unfastened her shoes. He handed her two slices of bread and some kind of meat, then sat the coffee pot amongst the coals. The man sat down on one end of the log and ate his meal.

They watched as steam rose from the spout of the coffee pot. He poured Sarah a cup.

"At least he's treating her decent," Clem whispered to Samuel.

"I hope he has taken good care of her. If he hasn't, he'll pay!"

"They've settled for the night, let's give them a half hour, then crawl closer," Clem directed.

The pair waited tensely.

"Okay, since you're on his side, you take him," Samuel whispered. "He's propped against that log. We'll try not to wake him until you've got your pistol at his head."

"Right and you get her, but don't scare her until I've got him, or she may wake him up too soon," Clem added.

"Signal me when you get ready to jump."

"Let's go," Clem said.

The pair crept forward, Samuel arranged himself to grab Sarah, Clem to reach over the log with his pistol at Adkisson's head. Clem's hand came down.

"Don't move, you're covered!" He held the gun on the hat over Adkisson's face. He reached his other hand to remove the covering to look into the man's face. Clem lifted the hat.

"Sam, he's not here!"

Samuel grabbed Sarah and moved her back behind several trees.

The three were stunned. Clem crouched and looked all around.

"Come on, I've got Sarah, let's move further away," Samuel directed.

"He must be hiding, I don't want him at our back. Keep going. I'll cover you." Clem said.

The three pulled back, reconnoitering as they kept going toward their horses. Often, Clem dropped behind to listen.

Sarah finally got her breath. "I knew God would send someone for me. I prayed and prayed for you all."

The moved closer to the horses.

"I prayed for him too," Sarah whispered.

"You prayed for Adkisson?" Samuel was incredulous.

"That's remarkable," Clem added.

"I've forgiven him for some of the things he did. I don't think he'll change, but he's in God's hands now. I tried to get him to change and turn me loose. Please let him go, that way, his blood won't be on our hands," she pleaded.

"Let's leave his old horse and get out of here," Clem said.

"We've been in this enemy hole long enough."

Samuel threw Sarah aboard the packhorse and the trio galloped away, Clem leading, Sarah in the middle and Samuel followed as rear guard.

After a few minutes, Sarah shouted, "How's Gideon?"

"He was in the Granger kitchen on a cot when we left," Samuel answered.

"He told us everything, so I think he'll be fine by the time we get back," Clem said.

They rode as fast as the horses could stand for the first two hours, then walked the next mile. When they stopped for a breather, Sarah had time to thank the pair.

"I knew God would send someone, but I had begun to think I might have to walk back from Texas," Sarah said.

"That's where you were headed?" Samuel asked.

"Yes, he thought he could join other southerners there and they'd have a *new south* all over again, with all that means," Sarah explained.

"We're sure glad you won't be a part of it," Clem remarked.

"Yes, I kept trying to get him to let me go. I told him he'd make better time without me, but he insisted that I go along with him. At first it was for his protection, then— he just hung on." Sarah was embarrassed by Adkisson's proposal and didn't relate that to her two friends. She looked away for a moment.

"I prayed for him, that surprised him. He asked me about God, but I'm not sure how much impression that made on him"

"I'd have a hard time praying for someone that took me hostage. I have to admire that in you," admitted Samuel.

"That's the goodness in you," Clem added.

"No. Like I told Mr. Adkisson, I think that's Christianity— and a woman speaking."

"What do you mean about the woman part?"

"He told me to be quiet on several occasions when I told him something he didn't want to hear. I told him that was the difference in men and women. *Men act, and women talk.* I still go along with my philosophy on this war we've been in."

"How's that?" Clem asked.

"If women were in control, we'd have talked and not shot each other. This thing would already be over."

"Guess she got us there, Sam."

"Yes, Sarah, you're probably right. Hate to admit it, but you are," Clem agreed.

᠃

The next four days were an uncomfortable time of riding and more riding. However, this time, the riders and horses were well fed. The men had brought along good trail food for themselves and Sarah. They made much better time than when they had traveled to the northwest.

When they arrived back in New Orleans, Sarah was in better condition than when they found her.

"I want to go see Gideon first. Then I'm going to soak and sleep for days."

"We'll see that a guard is posted near this house," Samuel said.

"When Sam takes the horses back to headquarters, he'll tell them you're back," Clem added. "I'll stay in the vicinity until the army can see to your safety."

"Tell them not to ask anything of me for several days. I'm too tired to even think." Sarah's head drooped.

"I don't know what they will want us to do next, but they may send Clem and me out on another job. We might even be at another location."

"We'll let you know, if we are to leave New Orleans," Clem added.

"You both know that I can't thank you enough. You were grand. I'll always be grateful. God bless you both. I know I'm being selfish, but I truly hope you will be here as long as we are."

"We'll bring Cleota back as soon as we can," Clem declared.

She kissed both men on the cheek, and ran across the grounds to Gideon's home.

The two men watched her go, then Samuel turned to leave.

Sarah spoke before she reached the fence, "Gideon? Gideon, where are you? I'm back."

A shadow rose up more slowly than usual, from his

regular place behind the Granger house. He had a white bandage over one eye.

"Oh, Gideon." Sarah placed her hands on either side of his face and drew him to her. She gently kissed the bandage over the spot where he had been injured and then placed her cheek on his uninjured one. Tears ran down both faces and mingled.

Sarah had to look at him again. She drew back and traced his tear with her thumb, picked up her skirt and gently dried his face.

"Gideon, you were so wonderful. You saved me from Mr. Adkisson and I'll never be able to thank you enough. You're such a wonderful boy. Oh, I love you, Gideon!"

"Me too, Miss Sarah." They stood together in a mutual embrace.

"Gideon, I've made up my mind. I'm going to buy you from Mr. Granger!"

"Oh, Missy, can youse?"

"We'll go now and ask. Is he here?"

"No, Ma'am. He ain't been here for weeks. I think he left New Orleans a long time ago."

"Well, we'll go right now and see if you can come and live with me at my house until he gets back. How about that?"

"Dat's fine, Missy."

The pair walked toward the Granger home. Later, they came out of the neighboring kitchen.

If Sarah could find Mr. Granger, their temporary arrangement would be finalized.

Sarah's grimy, mosquito bitten arm remained around Gideon's shoulders. They leaned into each other as they crossed the lawn. To most observers, the small pair looked near the same age.

In New Orleans

By April 27, 1862, General Benjamin Butler had been given military governorship of the conquered city of New Orleans after he and his troops had landed just north of Fort St. Philip.

Upon the Federal capture of New Orleans, all slaves of those disloyal to the Union had been freed.

An uneventful, almost happy, and relieved six weeks followed the trio's return to the city.

Sarah had Gideon to care for. She started his Bible and reading lessons. The boy ate like he'd never eaten before. A white scar remained where Adkisson had struck him while taking Sarah. Both Gideon and Sarah choose to ignore past problems and reveled in their newfound and companionable freedom.

The troops ceased guarding the house when martial law was established. General Butler reported New Orleans as a "city under the dominion of the mob."

When the United States flag was posted on the customhouse and city hall, the citizenry vented their anger and sorrow.

The female population reacted by pouring their chamber pots onto the soldiers below their second story windows and southern women spit on those they met on the streets.

Adverse civilian action brought *military reaction* from the occupying army. General Butler enacted his *Woman Order*, which allowed the arrest of any woman showing contempt for the occupying troops. These contemptuous women were to be classified *women of the town, plying their trade.*

General Butler also took over control of the town newspapers to prevent slanderous writings..

Sarah and Cleota, with the household staff stayed within the iron fence at the mansion. The streets of New Orleans were unsafe.

≈⋅

Today, Sarah sat alone under the magnolia tree and breathed a prayer to her Lord.

"Oh, God, thank you for giving me Gideon. Keep him strong and well. Help him to grow to love you, as I do. Thank you. Thank you for this peace and security that we feel right here in this house. End the war, so we can go back up the Mississippi and see my papa. I pray he's well again. Help me to live in the way you would have me to, and— deal with Montgomery. He needs you. Father—"

"Still praying for me, I see."

Sarah started, opened her eyes and stood from the stone bench. Her Bible fell from her lap, her hand went to her throat.

"I didn't know anyone was around," she said.

"Apparently," Adkisson spoke quietly.

"How did you get here?"

"I rode back. It took me a little longer than it did you, I see."

"Are you mocking me?" she asked.

"No, just thought I'd come back and see if you were well and— I see that you are. I've never seen you look more beautiful, Sarah." He breathed a sigh.

Sarah drew further away, "Why are you *really* here?"

"Everything I have, I left in this house. I had to come retrieve it, if I mean to make a new life for myself."

Her heart lurched, *His money? Please don't let it be me.*

"You need to take what you own and leave. Soldiers patrol here often, they will be by anytime," Sarah stated.

"Are you trying to get rid of me?" He spoke softly.

Sarah strained to hear him.

At that moment, Gideon came from the house. His head came up and he screamed as he launched himself at the young master. The man fended the youth off with his hands.

Sarah reached for Gideon and put herself in front of him. He was difficult to hold with his increasing strength.

"It's all right, Gideon, he's not going to hurt us this time. God won't let him," she soothed.

Adkisson spoke quickly, "You still believe that God can protect you? Believe it or not, I think he will. I will never hurt either of you again. I came back to tell you that I'm changing. Your little talks got to me, even though I didn't want to listen." He bowed and touched his hat to his shin, "Another conquest, Miss Sarah."

"Not my victory, but God's."

"You're right. I'm not all the way yet, but I'm getting there." He looked at the boy, "Forgive me, Gideon. I'm sorry that I hurt you and Miss Sarah. I know that's hard for you to believe, but I'd appreciate it if you'd accept my apology?"

"No, I ain't forgivin' you. You're Satan's."

"Nevertheless. I beg your pardon, but I must be going." He dismissed the boy and looked into Sarah's face, "I probably won't be back, but I thank you both. Here's my key to the gate and the house."

He reached out his hand. Sarah took the hand reluctantly, then quickly released it when he attempted to raise her hand to his lips. She stepped back.

"God speed you toward *Him*," she whispered.

Adkisson turned on his heel, placed his hat on his head and moved off quickly toward the house.

Sarah's eyes followed him for a moment, then she turned to Gideon and drew him into her arms. The pair trembled and held each other. Sarah rocked them both in a soothing maternal rhythm. A soft lullaby began in her throat and moved until it was not contained, the sound sprang from her lips in a joyous, soothing song.

From the back verandah, the young master listened. His eyes misted. *Thank you, for allowing me to know her.*

He moved as a shadow toward the carriage house and renewed flight.

The Mill of War Grinds Fine

Each area fought its own battles on its home playing field.

Back in Missouri, infamous Order Number 11 was a governmental attempt to control guerilla terrorist activities in Kansas and western Missouri. The balance of the state and Kansas attempted to absorb the 20,000 displaced and homeless resulting from the depopulation of the western counties in Missouri.

November 1, 1862, had brought on the emancipation of all slaves owned by other than loyal citizens of the Union and allowed the freed slaves to enter the military.

In New Orleans, when General Butler could not pacify the population of New Orleans, he was removed December 15, 1862, from the military governorship of New Orleans.

The population of New Orleans was not sorry to see his departure.

General Nathaniel Banks was made commander of the Army of the Gulf and assumed his occupation duties in and around New Orleans.

᠎

Months passed in New Orleans with little activity for the four undercover agents. Their friendship continued on a more normal level for young people. They had the protection of the occupying Union army and little need other than keeping their ears open for underground rebellious feelings in the communities.

General Banks attempted to clean up the civilian and governmental problems in New Orleans and delayed his departure for the Red River country for the army and navy's campaign toward Texas.

During the disastrous attempt and many narrow escapes, the Federal Fleet and the army returned unsuccessful in their attempted military victory to New Orleans and other fields of battle.

ê▲

Winter changed to spring. The seasons slid into the summer of 1863.

Sarah moved languidly in the summer heat and humidity. No one of the household worked any faster than absolutely necessary.

July sixth, in the morning heat, Clem informed Sarah of the latest development.

"The six week siege at Vicksburg has ended."

"Praise the Lord. I'm so glad. Those poor people must have suffered being shelled and having no fresh supplies coming in. Samuel told us they were living in caves in the hillsides to avoid the daily shelling," Sarah said.

"Our soldiers would suffer in this heat too. Lying out in those encampments and behind the fortifications must have been miserable. Some of those poor boys are still wearing wool uniforms," Clem stated.

"They all must have been miserable."

"General Pemberton surrendered on July fourth," Clem added.

"Independence Day! Hallelujah! Hope that has more meaning than just the surrender of Vicksburg," Sarah added.

"I think we're getting there. This thing should be over

with the Mississippi River cutting the secesh's supply lines and preventing the supplies from the west from being shipped east, and no northern or southern flow of supplies to the southern cause."

"Thanks for telling me. It's good to hear good news. If we can just hear the south surrender, then I'd be happy and we could go home."

"There have been big battles at Gettysburg, Pennsylvania. It seems that Lee may be returning toward the south. If that is true, the capitol at Washington has been saved again.

Clem looked into Sarah's face. His eyes became serious, "There's just one reason I don't want this war over."

"Clem!" she gasped.

"Then you'll go home and I'll never see you again."

"It's a small world, you can come to Missouri and visit us anytime you want. I know Papa will be glad to meet you. I've written him about my- *friends*, but I haven't been able to tell him any names. I'll be very happy to introduce all of you to my papa and then we can sit down and have a peaceful visit without any problems to worry about."

"Don't I wish," Clem turned back to wait on a customer who entered the door.

Captured

Samuel hurriedly walked up the front path. Twice he raised the heavy brass knocker and let it fall on the ornate front door.

Sarah entered the front hallway to answer his summons. She looked out the sidelight, then swung open the door.

"Samuel— come in."

"Sarah, I had to come tell you, Montgomery Adkisson has been captured. He's being held in a parish jail near Baton Rouge. He awaits trial and possible execution for his part in the rebellion."

She looked away for a moment.

He spoke again, "Sarah, are you all right?"

"Yes, I'm fine. Can we go see him?" she asked.

"Are you sure that's what you want to do?" he asked.

"Yes, I must."

"I'll check with the military court. I don't know if they will allow us to travel."

"Please, can you do that? I feel I should see him one more time."

"Why? Sarah, are you going soft on that man? I'm sorry, forget what I said. I'll get Clem and we'll be back as soon as we can."

"Samuel, he was so close to coming to God, I'd never forgive myself if he was executed without that chance."

"I see."

"Can you go immediately?" she asked.

"I can't promise you we'll be allowed to go, but if we are, yes, I'll go with you," Samuel cautioned.

"Thanks, you are a good friend, Samuel."

Samuel hugged her and turned to go.

"I'll be praying," she added.

"I thought you would."

Later, Sarah walked to the store, opened the door to the steps that led to the loft and spoke, "Clem, are you up there?"

Clem came down the stairs with his shirt sleeves rolled to the middle of his strong forearms.

"Sarah, it's good to see you." He looked into her face, then clasped her arm. They stood facing each other.

"You look worried, are you all right?" he asked.

"Montgomery Adkisson has been captured and is awaiting trial near Baton Rouge," she said.

"I know. I was afraid you'd hear," he commented.

She looked surprised. "Why would you say that?"

"Because I knew you were concerned for his soul. He apparently hasn't changed and I knew that would hurt you."

"Yes," she breathed. "I can't give up. Please understand. If I can, I must try to get him to come to Jesus of his own accord. I wouldn't forgive myself if I didn't use every opportunity the Lord gives me."

"I do understand— I've prayed too," he said.

"Thank you, Clem. If I get permission would you come too?"

"You'd have a hard time keeping me from it. Who else is going?"

"Samuel wants to go with me, if he can get permission."

"Just say when."

Sarah hugged Clem. "Thank you, I thought you'd say

yes."

"Kind of hard to turn you down, Sarah," his voice choked off.

"It's hard for me to turn God down."

"I know."

"I knew you'd understand," she whispered.

Clem wrapped his long arms around her, held her to him.

"I couldn't bear it if anything happened to you, Sarah."

"I feel the same about you and Samuel. You've both held my lifeline for the past two years."

"As little as you are, you've been more than that to me. You're a source of strength and power like I've never before known."

"I don't have any strength myself, it's from God."

"I love you Sarah."

"I love you too," she replied.

"I wish I believed you meant that in the way I do."

"I can't give you that answer. I don't know myself," she said.

"Good ole Sam. He's in there too, isn't he?"

"Yes I love you both," she said.

"I thought maybe by now you'd have an answer for us," he commented.

"I'm sorry, there's just too much going on. I'm confused. I've asked God's help, but so far—   ," her voice trailed off.

"I won't press you. After all, you're worth waiting for."

She gave him a playful squeeze, "Thank you. Let me know if you hear from Samuel when we can head toward Baton Rouge." She turned to leave, "Clem, please pray for Montgomery."

"I will— for all of us, Sarah."

Sarah turned away with a tear of gratitude on her cheek.

Under the shade of the overhanging trees on the boardwalk she prayed as she walked toward home.

Lord, thank you for my good friends. Please draw Montgomery to You. He may be executed, please don't let him go to hell.

A voice sounded in her heart, *I'm always here, it's his choice.*

Sarah breathed her reply. *May I accept your will, but I won't stop asking.*

Prison Visitors

The silent young guard had issued his directive to the trio, "I can only allow the prisoner one visitor and that one will have to be searched before he is admitted."

Wishing to protect Sarah, Samuel spoke first. "We've been cleared by the military governor's office from New Orleans. We all worked for the Union throughout the war, there is no question about our loyalty."

"I'm sorry, Sir, I have my orders."

Clem spoke, "Thanks, we're glad you obey. We'll decide amongst ourselves who will go in. Sarah and Sam, let's discuss this outside."

The three gathered on the boardwalk.

"Sarah, we can't allow you to be searched. One of us will go see Adkisson," Clem voiced the two men's concern.

"I was the one with him across Louisiana and I think I can make more headway with him than either of you. I don't mind the search, since that's the only way I can get in," Sarah stated.

"I have to admit he will probably be more receptive to your suggestions than to either of ours, much as I hate to admit it," Clem agreed.

"I don't like it, but I think Clem's right. All right, Sarah, if you must, you must," Samuel said.

The group turned back to the soldier.

The young guard spoke with embarrassment, "We have the jailer's wife, she'll take you into their private rooms. You can carry nothing into the jail, but your person."

"I have a New Testament for the prisoner, please allow me to take that to him. I feel that God would wish him to have this little volume," she said.

"I don't know— "

"Oh, please."

"I'll take the book to my commander, when you come back, I'll tell you what he says."

He riffled the pages of the small pocket New Testament, held it by the binding and shook it, then carried it to the front offices.

After the search, Sarah came back into the hallway of the jail. The young jailer returned carrying the New Testament. The back and the flyleaf had been torn loose in their search.

"He says this is okay to take to the prisoner," he said.

Sarah smoothed the little volume reverently between her hands, then clasped it to her heart.

"I'm ready to see Mr. Adkisson now, if I might." She straightened her spine.

"Come along." The guard led the way.

She recognized the occupant of the cell. Montgomery Adkisson sat upon his bunk with his head in his hands.

Sarah approached, placed her hands on the bars and spoke softly with apology in her voice, "How are you?"

His head jerked up, he stared at the young silhouette clinging to the bars of his cell.

"How did you find me?" he asked.

"It wasn't hard. I quote from the New Orleans Sentinel put out by the military government, *Prominent New Orleans Conspirator Arrested.*"

"Oh, I suppose I did make a name for myself." His voice sounded dead.

"Yes," she said.

"It's not something I'm proud of anymore."

"Really? I'm glad."

"You're glad that I'm in this cell and may be executed for my part in the attempted overthrow of a tyrannical government?" he asked.

"That's what I worked for," Sarah said.

"Yes, I forgot. You did come to New Orleans to ensnare the horrible crooks that killed your fiancée," he said.

"Yes, but I'd prefer if we could forget that and be friends," she said.

"I should hate you, but I don't. Just as you should hate me, but you now say you don't," Adkisson said.

"If God can forgive you, I can hardly do less," Sarah replied.

"Why did I listen to you? Before you came, I was successful and I had a rich life. I could have been important in the new nation of the south, but you came along. . . "

"Success depends on what you're looking for." She looked at him pointedly, "Are you happy?"

"No, I'm not. You saw to that with your constant talk of God, you lived it too. At least, I'm no longer indifferent to your God. I hope you're satisfied, I'm in constant torment and this cell only adds to that. I can't get away from myself— or God."

"I think that's good."

He clawed his hand through his hair, "That's good. How can you sentence a person to this?"

"Exactly what are you sentenced to?" she asked.

"Why couldn't you just love me and leave my soul alone?" he asked.

"You are not *you* without your soul."

"So you've made me believe."

"Do you believe anything else about God?" Sarah asked.

"I'm not sure. I always took care of myself. Now, the enemy has seen that I can't do that." He searched her face, "If I could just get out of here, I'd be all right." He looked at her speculatively, then lowered his voice, "You could help me get away."

"No, I couldn't do that. You know why I went to New Orleans— what I did to stop you and your friends before you could hurt anyone else."

"Do you hate me so?" he asked.

She looked down considering, "No, my God won't let me hate you any longer. I hate what you did, but— "

A ray of hope shown in his eyes, "Could you ever love me?"

"Not in the way you want."

He turned away, "I know, I know! You love me as a brother in Christ."

"I love you as another of God's creations, but I don't think I could ever love you in any other way."

"You're being hypocritical!" he stated.

"No, you lost that kind of respect from me, when you took another's life. I can't permit that."

"I thought God said, *'Vengeance is mine'*?"

"He did," she said.

"Why do you have to help him?"

"That's hard to explain."

He dropped onto the cot in his cell. Very still for a moment, a sigh escaped him.

"I'm sorry, that's not fair. I know that I've done wrong and I am sorry for it. You've made me think about God. I can't take care of myself any longer and right now, I'm not sure I want to try," he said.

"I'm sorry you're down and suffering so miserably, but this can be to your advantage—"

"How's that?" he asked.

"Until you got into a position where you had to trust in God, you've put him aside. Now you will have to consider him and make a decision."

"As much as I hate to agree with you, I think you may be right this time."

"You can use this time to your advantage. The guard allowed me to bring you this." She reached her hand into the cell. On her small palm, lay the New Testament. "Take it. I pray it brings you peace."

"Are you sure this is allowed?"

"Yes, they've thoroughly examined it. I'm sorry that it's torn, but they had to see if I was smuggling you an escape weapon. *It is an escape*, but not one dangerous to others," she said.

Adkisson stood slowly, took a step closer and reached for her hand. He brought it to his lips. She didn't resist, but left her hand in his. He looked at her palm as it lay quiet as a dead bird.

He took a breath. "*Calm*, you're always so calm. I'd like it better if you had some reaction to me."

"I do, I plead with God for your soul constantly," she breathed.

"I know you do, but that's not what I want."

She ignored his last remark.

The guard rattled the bars of the hall door. "Miss, you've got to leave now."

"Please read the New Testament. If you don't understand something, you could ask the chaplain."

"Won't you come again? I'd rather ask you."

"I'm not sure— I'll try."

"That's all I can ask. Good-by, fair lady." He released her hand and turned aside.

She turned. He watched her leave him, a haunted expression on his face. With his hands, he gripped the bars, placed his cheek against the cold steel.

As the guard opened the door, she looked back, raised her hand once more to him. Her skirts swished in the silence as she exited.

The closing door echoed with a dull clang.

She heard a muted groan through the peephole on the door. She walked away, praying.

Samuel and Clem didn't question her when she came from the jail with her set face. Clem untied the horses and held the reins. Samuel placed his hands on his bent knee for her.

Sarah climbed silently aboard, subdued. "Thank you." She pulled the reins and turned the horse aside.

The two men looked at each other over the backs of their horses and mounted up. The three skirted the populated areas and rode back toward headquarters in New Orleans.

Finally, Sarah turned to look at first one then the other. "At least he's thinking about God now."

"Is that what you talked about?"

"Mostly."

"I'm surprised he didn't try to convince you to get him out?"

"He did mention that briefly, but he knows I won't help him in that way," she answered.

"Were you able to help him in other ways?" Clem asked.

"I think maybe I was. If God and I keep adding straws, surely we'll get through to him. He's a whole lot closer than he used to be."

"I hope you're right," Samuel added.

"Yes, about all we can do for him now is pray," Clem said.

"I've been doing that ever since he ran from New Orleans," Sarah replied.

"We were doin' the same out here," Samuel added.

"When?"

"While you were inside," he replied.

"And when he was on the run with you," Clem added.

Tears sprang to her eyes, she cleared her throat, "You are both so good to me. I'll never be able to thank you enough."

Samuel spoke, "We're not askin' for your thanks."

They rode in silence.

Samuel dropped further and further behind Clem and Sarah on the narrow woods trail. He spoke to the air. "Sarah, I can't speak for him, but I love you. I'm not askin' for your thanks, I want your love."

The lead pair rode on, oblivious to his declaration.

ॐ

Much later, Samuel spoke to Sarah, "Are things settled enough that I can come calling now?"

"Why not? New Orleans is becoming so quiet, there isn't much else to do."

"I don't want to come just because you can't think of anything better. I want to come because you want me to."

"I'm sorry, I didn't mean to sound as if I didn't want you to come. I just found visiting one of God's creations in jail rather depressing," Sarah sighed.

"I agree with you, it is depressing, but he choose which side to fight for — and he wasn't very reputable about it. I say we let martial justice— and God handle him."

Clem rode closer.

Sarah sighed, "You're right, but it's hard to see such a waste of human abilities."

"You planted a seed, you'll have to let God make it grow," Clem added.

"Yes, and you gave him a New Testament. God is giving him a choice, Adkisson will have to make the best use of it," Samuel added.

"Like God, we won't force him to it."

"You both are right, but I still can't stop praying for him," Sarah said.

"No, we can all do that," Samuel said.

"Would you like to pray together as we ride along?" Clem asked.

"Yes."

They rode through a country lane between old oaks with Spanish moss draped over the limbs. Sarah shivered and drew her shawl closer.

Clem spoke first, "I'll keep a look out while you two pray. Sam, why don't you start?"

The three rode with quiet murmured prayers rising from their hearts.

When Samuel and Sarah had exhausted their pleas, Clem took up the lament.

Amnesty For Almost All

Months later, Sarah received a letter in a soiled envelope with marks foreign to her. She tore it open, wondering from whence it came.

Dearest Sarah,

Through a legal fluke and with general amnesty, I have escaped the firing squad or the gallows.

I did not pull the trigger that killed your fiancée and injured your family members, but I was involved and take responsibility.

In my old life, I would have never thought I'd be telling you this, but your unveiling my treachery was the best thing that ever happened to me. I have you to thank for your persistence in telling me of Jesus Christ. You showed me how a Christian should live, even in trying circumstances, many of which I am responsible for.

I've made my peace with God.

Jesus and I have gone down through Mexico. I'll probably never see you again on this earth, but I will see you one day in heaven.

Forgive me for all the hurt I caused you, even before I kidnaped you. Please accept my apologies if I continued to hurt you. I am genuinely repentant. I know you like that word and all its meanings.

God willing, I will spend my life making up for the

evil I did you and yours, but it will be helping others in another land. This time I will be helping those with darker skin than my own and I will treasure each soul I meet. Knowing your feelings on this subject, I am assured you will approve of this change in my character.

I'm finished in the southern part of the United States. I never plan to return there.

I pray only the best for you. May you have a good life and find a good God-fearing man to share your life, if that's what you wish. I regret that it could not be me, but I damaged that relationship before it began. I can blame only myself for my sins.

I never wish to cause you worry or sorrow again, please believe me in this. I thank you for your forgiveness and all that you mean in my life. If it were not for Jesus Christ, I could call you my savior, but I know that is not what you would wish.

I will not fully sign this message, to prevent you further grief.

My Love and Admiration Always, MA.
P.S.

Please offer my regrets to your servant for me. I'm sorry for the way I treated her and Gideon too.

I can't say it often enough, My love always, MA.

The letter was postmarked, *Mexico City.*

Sarah's hand rose to a tear that sparkled on her cheek.

Thank you Lord. He really has changed, before he would never have asked for forgiveness from Cleota or Gideon. Be with him. I'm glad for him, help him live well and in your will henceforth. I pray he'll find a good ministry with a good and full life with many converts to You, Father. May Jesus' will be done in his entire life. Amen

Back Home in Missouri
September 1864

Clem hurried to meet Sarah at the door of the store.

"Did you know Fort Davidson had been blown up?" he asked.

"Fort Davidson, in Missouri?" she asked.

"My contact said the small group of Federal soldiers were surrounded. They crept out during the night, then blew the magazine rather than allow General Price's Confederates to capture them."

"I know many of those strong Federalists in the Arcadian Valley. Was anyone hurt?" Sarah asked.

Clem took her arm. "There weren't many Federal casualties, but hordes from the Rebels. They outnumbered those in the fort and left little choice for our friends but to fight them off when they charged against those inside the breastworks."

"I'm glad they got out safely. I would guess there was no reason to go down with their sinking ship," she said.

"Yes, they'll live to fight another day," Clem replied.

"All this makes me homesick for my friends who live there. Papa and I used to go there often to visit and buy ore or charcoal. They are one of Papa's largest suppliers. Did the Rebels get control of the mines?" she asked.

"I'm sorry, I don't have an answer to that question," Clem stated.

"I guess there's not much we can do about it from here."

"Keep praying," Clem said.

"Yes, I do that everyday," Sarah replied.

Some Months Later

Clem hailed Sarah when she entered the store, "Come back here, I have something to tell you."

"Have you heard good news?" she asked.

"I imagine you will think it so."

"Don't make me wait, what is it?" Sarah asked.

"One of our contacts said that all the slaves in Missouri have been freed. It came through Union General William S. Rosecrans, commander of the Department of Missouri, after Missouri's Emancipation Ordinance passed January 11," he said.

"It must be true then and I'm so glad." She hugged Clem.

"I should give you more good news if this is the way you react,"

"It's so good to hear something good from home, I couldn't contain myself, but we'd better get back out front or someone will come looking for you and spoil our reputations," Sarah smoothed her skirts and went through the storeroom door.

She looked around. No one was in the store.

"God took care of us that time too but it's getting so we don't have to worry so much about appearances any longer," she said.

"You're right," he laughed.

Honorably Discharged

"We're free! They have no more need of us in New Orleans or anywhere in the south." Samuel relayed the message to Sarah, Cleota and Clem as they sat in the mansion's kitchen sipping newly imported coffee. "We've done such good work, they're discharging all of us."

Gideon slept on the cot next to the wall.

The group sobered as they pondered parting.

"When will you leave?" Clem questioned Sarah.

"Cleota and I haven't had time to think about it. Why don't you two come with us? We'll all go to Missouri. My father would give you jobs if you'd like. We could go together. I don't want to lose contact with either of you." She reached for the two men's hands.

"What do you think, Clem?"

"Might be a good trip. We all need a rest after the past several years. I'm not sure if I'm ready to go home yet," Clem stirred restlessly.

"Sounds good to me, when do you want to start?" Samuel asked.

"Let's see if we can catch a boat up the Mississippi River. I'm sure my father's name would still carry some weight," Sarah enthused.

"If it doesn't, the military probably owes us passage. One way or the other we should be able to go north."

Samuel rose. "Let me check. I'll get back to you four,

be seeing you as soon as I know something."

"Yes, Sir. You do that," Cleota added.

Sarah rose from the table, "Cleota, let's start packing our things and get ready. I'm anxious to see my papa."

"Yes, Ma'am. Sure hope he's fared better while we've been gone all these years. It's been hard to tell by his letters, even though he's said he is doing well."

⅋

While they packed their meager belongings into a trunk for shipment, Sarah and Cleota sang the rousing *Battle Hymn of the Republic* as their celebratory victory song.

Samuel returned with disheartening news, "If the Mississippi River was open to civilian traffic, that would be the easiest way, but the general said the army won't give us that choice if we wish to leave soon."

"I hope the Mississippi will be open for civilian trade very soon," Sarah added.

"That will happen, I   hope," Cleota added her thoughts.

Samuel came in the door with a whoop. "General Banks said we could board the *Memphis* on Sunday afternoon at three, if that suits everyone?"

"How far does she go?" Sarah questioned.

"The *Memphis* goes around Florida and up the east coast. He'll give us a voucher for any place under Union control or if we want to board a different boat. I asked but he won't let us travel the Mississippi River."

Sarah thought aloud, "When we go up the coast we wouldn't want to disembark until we got as far north as Washington, D.C. Philadelphia would be even better. Then we'd have to go overland and finally to a boat going toward the Mississippi River."

"Cleota, and I used to take several routes with Papa. Suitable routes? Let's see, I don't know how much the train tracks have suffered."

"We haven't been that way since the war got so rough. Things may have changed," Cleota commented.

"Once we get back to the Ohio River, then to the Mississippi River and steam north, we can coast straight into St. Louis," Sarah reminded the trio.

"They've got us there. The ladies sure know more about the Union than I do," Samuel said.

"You're right, guess we'll have to try it and see for ourselves," added Clem.

Home Again, Home Again

The four friends departed New Orleans the first Sunday afternoon, in May, 1865, to return to their post-civil war, northern world. The Yankees had freed all the slaves of New Orleans when they occupied the city and the Emancipation Proclamation had completed the job in all seceded areas of the south. Now with Lee's surrender, all slaves were granted their freedom state by state as their governments met in their respective state conventions .

The uneducated and ill-prepared freed women and men faced new problems, but Gideon was safe with Sarah. The four friends chose to take the boy along when they started to Sarah's home in Missouri.

Upon their arrival in St. Louis, they found Sarah's father much recovered. In his great relief and happiness to see the five, he offered Samuel and Clem jobs with the iron foundry. Clem took the job, but Samuel declined and went off to acquire a job with the city marshal's office.

Both young men bunked in the single quarters at the foundry and ate frequent meals with Sarah's family. Gideon slept in his own room in the main dwelling. He still shadowed Sarah, and did small jobs for the household..

One Sunday afternoon, Sarah stretched and commented after a sumptuous meal.

"I haven't felt so relaxed in years. It seems that life *may* actually resume with some normalcy. We've got plenty to eat; enough work to keep us busy; and Papa's feeling better. It's wonderful."

"Life is getting boring, isn't it?" Samuel commented.

"Boring? How can you say that?" Clem answered.

"I was joking, life isn't boring, but much quieter than it has been for some time," Samuel said.

"I, for one, am ready for peace and quiet. It didn't come too soon. *War is tiring*," Sarah added.

"And we didn't even fight battles. Can you imagine what that would have been like?" Samuel added.

Cleota fidgeted, "I got something on my mind, Miss Sarah, could I speak to you in private?"

"Certainly, Cleota, let's go into the sitting room." She turned back to the gentlemen, "You men stay here and enjoy yourselves."

She turned to her friend, "What is it Cleota?"

"Can I bring Moses Blanks to St. Louis?"

"*Who* is Moses Blanks?"

"He lived near me in New Orleans. We got cozy and I'd like to bring him here. Do you think your father would approve?"

A light sprang into Sarah's eyes. "The only way to find out is to ask him. Let's do that right now."

Sarah opened the door, "Papa, could you come in here for a minute?"

"Young ladies, what do you have on your minds?" he asked.

"Cleota wants to bring her friend, Moses Blanks, to St. Louis."

"Cleota, do you want to go back to New Orleans?"

"No sir, there's not much there for colored folk, but I'd like to bring Moses up here," she said.

"If you speak for him, I'm sure he's all right. I'll send

him passage. Do you have an address for him?" Mr. Turner asked.

"I've been writing him. We miss each other. I'd appreciate it if you'd give him a job for a while, but we got some money saved. I can pay his passage," Cleota said.

"I'm grateful to you, Cleota. I can't see you spending your money on his passage. I insist in giving you a bonus for the years you spent in New Orleans taking care of my little girl."

"First, Miss Sarah isn't any little girl and the government paid me well, I wouldn't want to be paid twice."

"Consider it a gift then. You deserve it. You've given loyalty to our family since you first came to be with us. I'm sure you put our needs above your own many times, this is the least I can do for you," he said.

"As a Christian sister, I can accept it, but call it a *wedding* present," Cleota said.

"You're in love! Why didn't you tell me, Cleota?" Sarah squealed and grabbed her friend in a bear hug.

Cleota ducked her head. "Old people don't go around talking about love, like some of you young folk."

"You're not old!" Sarah exclaimed.

"No, I'm only forty-one. I've got plenty of life left."

Sarah grabbed Cleota and danced her in a circle.

Three young men poked their heads around the door facing.

"What's going on in here?" Clem asked.

"Yes, you left us one by one, then you're having a party in here." Samuel turned to the other young men. "They didn't invite us, suppose we ought to leave?" he joked.

"Come on and join the party. Cleota has some wonderful news for us all," Richard Turner waved the three into the room.

"Go ahead, tell them," Sarah prompted.

Cleota looked first at one, then the other. They all

waited.

"If you won't tell them, can I?" Sarah begged.

"Go ahead, Missy, you been tellin' my secrets all your life."

"Cleota is bringing her fiancée to St. Louis and they are going to get married!" Sarah squealed.

The young males opened their mouths, but no sound came out.

"They're speechless for once. You really got them this time, Cleota," Sarah laughed.

Clem was the first to speak. "Congratulations to you Cleota, why didn't you tell us before?"

"Yes," Sarah put in, "we could have brought him with us when we came. He wouldn't have to come alone then."

"Some people have to be apart to help make up their minds," Cleota said.

"And some don't. Sarah, let's make it a double wedding," Samuel said with a teasing grin.

Sarah smiled back at both young men.

"I can't think of any others that are ready to make it a double wedding. Can you, Clem?"

"Yes, but not the one Samuel is thinking of," Clem said.

"I think it's about time we changed the subject." Sarah turned to Cleota, "Do you have a date set?"

"Not until Moses arrives. We don't know how long that will take. When he gets here, I'll get his wants on a date. Now shoo, you young folks, that's enough about me." She turned to a her long-time friend and boss, "Mr. Turner, you want some more coffee?"

Happiness lit the faces of the three young adult members of the party.

"Let's go for a walk," Sarah said.

"Yes, it's time to walk off some of that pie that Cleota baked to go with our coffee. Gideon, want to come along?"

Clem asked.

"No, thank yah, Mr. Clem. I'm going to help Mr. Turner."

One young man on either side of Sarah, they linked arms and walked around the lake on the foundry grounds.

"I was serious when I said we could have a double wedding," Samuel prompted.

"I was too," Clem said.

"What am I going to do with you two?" Sarah feigned horror.

"Too bad it isn't legal to have two husbands, then you wouldn't have to decide between us," Samuel laughed.

"Even though there were a few multiple spouses in the Bible, I don't agree with that. It's one man, one woman for life, when I get married," said Clem.

"Me too." Sarah quietly answered.

"You both know me well enough to know that's what I want too," Samuel agreed.

"Yes, we're doomed to go through life, until we find that one and only." Sarah grew quiet, "I thought I had him once, but it wasn't to be."

"People never know what is going to happen next. Life can be uncertain at best," Clem attempted comfort.

"Yes, that's why I'm so glad we are all Christians. No matter what happens, eventually we will see each other again," Sarah said.

"You're right there. Ole Adkisson too. Never thought I'd be glad to see him again. God certainly can change things fast," Samuel added.

"Sometimes I felt so very alone in New Orleans. You were both there for me, but not in the same house. *I always had to be on guard*. That was so hard. I couldn't even act my age," Sarah said.

"Well, we're not getting any younger, better make up

your mind before much longer, or we'll all be too old to walk down the aisle," Samuel said.

"You two make it harder every day. I ought to toss you both over and find someone new," Sarah laughed.

"Please don't," Clem pleaded.

"I agree on that," Samuel said.

Sarah ignored their comments. "It might take me years to get as well acquainted with someone new. I'd never see them under such adverse circumstances as I've seen you two." She looked first at one and then the other carefully. "You know, you both passed with flying colors. You're good ones to be with in tough times, you're both very handsome, you are both gentlemen—"

"Ma'am, you're embarrassing us. Isn't she, Clem?"

"Sure are, Ma'am."

Seriousness was lost in the night. The three strolled on, enjoying their friendship.

Later, when Cleota and Sarah prepared for bed.

"Miss Sarah, you got two wonderful young men there. Are you going to put them out of their misery one of these days?"

"I'd like to Cleota. I want a husband and a family very soon, but I love them both. I lean toward choosing one, then I change and lean the other way. Until I'm sure, I can't make a mistake with either one of them. God hasn't helped me on this decision. I keep asking. I'm getting impatient, but I'm afraid to make the choice on my own."

"Maybe it would help if we named their characteristics?"

"You start, Cleota."

"Mr. Sam got beautiful eyes. Mr. Clem got beautiful hair."

"Get serious, they are equally handsome, go deeper, you know I won't be swayed by a pretty face," Sarah said.

"But it don't hurt," Cleota said.

"Guess not, but that's not the deciding factor."

"I'll skip the outward appearance and we'll go inside. Mr. Sam laughs. Mr. Clem is serious sometimes—," Cleota enumerated qualities.

"I'll put that down. They both laugh, they've both got serious sides to their natures," Sarah wrote.

"What about their faith? Mr. Clem seems closer to God."

"That's hard to judge in another, Clem seems more serious in his faith, but that's not the only way to judge something like that. I see other signs from Samuel, so I think they are about equal there too."

"We're not getting far are we?" Cleota commented.

"No, that's been my trouble all along. They are both such good men, in their own way. I haven't been able to decide which I love the most," Sarah lamented.

"Could you be happy with either one of them?"

"Yes, I think I could."

"Does one of them give you the shivers?" Cleota asked.

"What do you mean?"

"Moses gives me the shivers. I just quiver all over inside when he comes around."

"Hum? I'm not sure about that one," Sarah said.

"I think you need that shiver to light your fire before you get married."

"I thought I had that with my fiancée, but it's been so long, it's hard for me to remember."

"I guess you are going to have to give yourself some more time." Cleota continued, " I know! Did either of them ever kiss you?"

"Yes, Samuel kissed my hands the first time he brought me home from visiting you at the fish shack."

"Well, what did it do for you?"

"It was wonderful. I felt— warm— and safe, like I hadn't for a long while. You were gone and I was afraid."

"That was good, but not a sure test. Maybe any man giving you a warm hand then, would have felt safe."

"When I went in that night, Montgomery Adkisson was waiting for me."

"Did he give you that shiver?" Cleota questioned.

"If I hadn't known so much about him, he might have. I had a hard time with his feelings toward slaves and some other things, but he did change. If we had been under more normal circumstances, and out of slavery, he might have. Before he became a Christian, in my heart, I knew he was cruel and he didn't care much for others. Why would God let me have a shiver over someone like that? I couldn't have married him, even if he'd wanted me to at the time."

"*At the time*, what do you mean?" Cleota asked.

"He did ask me to go with him to Texas and start a new life," Sarah said.

"Married?" Cleota asked.

"Yes."

"Did you think about it?"

"I couldn't, he wasn't a Christian and he hadn't changed at that time."

"Do you think thoughts of him might be in the way of you getting serious about Samuel or Clem?" Cleota asked.

"No. More than anything, I think they get into each others' way. If I had only one of them at a time, I think I could make up my mind. Usually, we're all together and it's hard to talk seriously with *anyone* under those circumstances," Sarah explained.

"You can't just make up your mind, you have to have your heart in it too."

"I know. Guess we'll just have to pray some more about it. *Lord, give me patience, and do it now!*" Sarah exclaimed.

"In His time, in His time. You remember that a thousand years is as the twinkling of an eye to God," Cleota said.

"Oh, please, don't make me wait a thousand years!" Sarah sighed.

"Go on girl, get in that bed and let me tuck you in, like I used to when you was little bitty." Cleota patted the covers, "You little bitty now." She reached up and tweaked Sarah's turned up nose.

Sarah looked at Cleota from under the covers. "Cleota, you're too good to me. I guess it's selfish of me, but I hope you and Moses don't decide to move away after you're married."

"We won't honey. Your papa said he'd give Moses a job and that'll guarantee we stay around close. Sides, you're family. Now you get to sleep," Cleota said.

Cleota blew out the candle and retreated to her room.

Sarah was left to mull over her situation with her Lord. She drifted off to sleep without an answer to her dilemma.

The next morning, she had a plan. *I'll introduce both of them to some available girls, then I'll see how they act. If one of them goes off with another girl, I'll know he wouldn't have been true to me.*

"Papa, I've decided to have some parties. Don't get too upset if young people are around all the time. I'll be sure they behave themselves. If you want, you can come to the parties, or retire to your own wing to relax."

"Are you trying to get rid of me during your parties?" her papa asked.

"No, I'm just trying to get some answers for myself," Sarah said.

Her father looked confused. He murmured to himself as he limped from the room, "Parties to get answers for herself, hummm? Strange. Never could figure out a woman."

Sorry, Papa, but I'm confused too. Guess I should have asked him which of the two he preferred, but that might not be fair to him.

❧

Cleota's Moses appeared on the scene and a quiet wedding occurred on Sunday afternoon. That evening after dinner, the happy pair disappeared into their suite. Sarah made it clear that no one was to disturb them until they chose to rejoin the family for meals.

❧

Two days later, Samuel and Clem joked at the dinner table.

"I think we should shivaree them. How about it?"

"What's a shivaree?" Clem asked.

"The neighbors come, shoot off their guns, make noise and get the couple out of bed. Then they make the groom pull his bride around in a buggy, or wheel her in a wheelbarrow. Generally, the neighbors make a nuisance of themselves, then the couple has to treat them with a meal, or something to get them to leave," Samuel replied.

"It's fun, but I think it's kind of cruel too," Sarah commented.

"It is fun. Usually, the neighbors bring them presents too, so they get compensated," Samuel answered.

"I think it would scare 'em," Gideon commented.

"I think it would be embarrassing," Sarah said.

"Depends. Some neighbors are more of a nuisance than others, and some get drunk, that doesn't help," Samuel said.

"Well, I don't think it should be taken too far. It might get out of hand," Sarah added.

"I expect since Moses has been a slave, it wouldn't be much fun for them. It *might* scare him," Clem said.

"I don't think we should do it," Sarah said.

"You're probably right there," Samuel conceded.

"You won't do it, will you?" Sarah asked Samuel.

"No, we won't do it. I hadn't thought about Moses being scared, but we won't take that chance," he agreed. "We don't want to hurt Cleota and Moses."

After midnight, Sarah was blasted awake by the sound of gunfire. She sat up in bed, startled out of a sound sleep.

"Oh, no. The boys are shivareeing Cleota and Moses after they said they wouldn't. Oh, God, please don't let anything bad happen." Sarah grabbed her long coat as she ran from her room. She buttoned the front as she flew down the hallway toward Cleota and Moses' suite.

As she came into sight of their door, she saw a white-clad figure grappling with another man. She leaped onto the figure and attempted to tear the two apart.

"Samuel? Samuel, if that's you, you are in serious trouble! Let go, quit right now," she screeched in the man's ear.

The figure let Moses go and turned to the menace at his back. He grabbed Sarah's arms and ripped her hands from his robe.

A snarly voice sounded in her ear. "Let go lady, or you'll get yours!"

Not Samuel's voice. Thank God. Please don't let him be involved.

The man set her aside and fled down the hallway and out the door, robes flying behind him.

Samuel and Clem entered from the opposite end of the porch, followed closely by Gideon.

"What's going on here?" Samuel asked.

"Someone was in the house. I'm so glad it wasn't you two," Sarah said.

"What do you mean?" Clem asked.

"I was afraid you were shivareeing Cleota and Moses."

"No, we weren't involved, but someone was. There's

a torch on the front lawn," Samuel said.

"Some white-robed men ran when we came from the bunkhouse," Clem replied.

Samuel rubbed his overnight stubble, "Someone meant to scare Moses and Cleota. Hurry and see if they're frightened or injured!"

"Cleota? Cleota, it's me, with Samuel and Clem. Let us in," Sarah pleaded.

The lock clicked.

"Are you all right?" Clem asked.

"Yes, Sir, we are fine, but no thanks to them." The door rattled and Cleota stood majestically with a chair leg in her hands. "I knew my family would come, I pulled the shutters too, hid Moses in the cupboard, and locked the door, after you got that man off him."

"And armed yourself. Good for you, Cleota," Sarah said.

She took the broom and brushed up broken shards of glass.

"Here, let me help you get this broken glass off the floor and tidy this place," Clem offered.

"Cleota, why don't you and Moses go to my room for the night? I'll sleep on the love seat. If they know where your room is, they may come back," Sarah directed.

"That's not necessary," Cleota said.

Clem was taking over. "Yes it is. Sam and I will stand guard tonight. If they come back, we'll get them."

"I doubt they will try it again. I don't think they knew how many would come to your rescue," Samuel said.

"We'll go back outside and scout around," Clem directed.

Sarah took Cleota and Moses by their elbows, "Come on, Cleota and Moses. Let's get out of this cold draft before we catch our death," Sarah led the pair down the dark hallway and into her room. She closed the shutters on the window, checked the latch on the door and grabbed a blanket from the quilt rack at the foot of her bed.

"I'll leave you two. If you need anything, I'll be in the sitting room. Good night. I hope we can all get some sleep after this."

"Thank you, Miss, but it ain't likely," Moses spoke for the first time.

"We won't let them hurt you. You're in the north now, Moses."

"Hatred don't know no boundaries, Miss Sarah."

"I'll be praying. God is stronger than any army they can raise," Sarah said.

"Yes 'em."

Sarah pulled the door too after herself. "Now, lock it from the inside." She heard the bolt shoved through the hasp. "I'll see you in the morning. Rest easy."

"Good night," Cleota answered.

Sarah turned into a warm body. "Gideon, can't you sleep?"

"No, Ma'am, I'm goin' to stay with you," he said.

"It won't be very comfortable. Let me get the throw off the piano. I'll use that and you can have this quilt."

Sarah placed Gideon's quilt on the fainting couch and patted it to show Gideon his bed was ready. The growing boy sat on the edge.

"Lay down, I'll tuck you in. Did your momma do that when you were little?" Sarah asked.

"I don't 'member my momma," Gideon said.

"I'm sorry." Sarah's voice caught, "My mother died when I was three, I know how it feels to not have a mother. Cleota tucked me in after that. She still does sometimes," she said.

"Wish you'd been my momma all the time," Gideon replied.

"I'd be a little too young to be your mother, but I'll be

glad to act the part now, if you like?"

"Yes 'em, I do."

"Okay, put your head here on the pillow and I'll sing you a lullaby." Sarah started to hum, then broke into a soft lullaby.

Clem sat on the porch below their window, where he stationed himself after the intruders left. He could hear her soft voice as she ministered to Gideon.

She's so beautiful, inside and out. Please, let her fall in love with me. I need her so. He continued to watch over Sarah and Gideon as the night passed quietly.

ૐ

Two months later, Cleota looked at Sarah's paper. "What are you doing?"

"I'm keeping score on Samuel and Clem," Sarah answered.

"Humm, is that totally fair?"

"No, but I still haven't come up with any other method."

Cleota's curiosity got the best of her. "Well, who's ahead?"

"Let's see, I'll tally them up. One, two, eight, ten. One, three, twelve. Well, so far Clem's ahead."

"Is that what your head says, or your heart?"

"Guess it's my head," Sarah answered.

"Does your heart agree?"

"Can't tell, yet."

"How do you feel about your score?"

"I don't like doing it," Sarah commented.

"Well, then don't. We were funnin' the other night, but that's not a good measure. You know the Lord says, *'Judge not, that yeh be not judged'.*"

"I know, but I'm just so frustrated, I'd like to get on with my life." Sarah sighed.

"I don't know what to tell you."

"I've about decided to go somewhere away from them and see who I miss the most," Sarah commented.

"That might work, it did for me and Moses."

"Are you happy, Cleota?"

"I'm really happy, truly happy. I didn't know what it was to be happy before. I had a good life but it's not like having someone of your very own," Cleota said.

Sarah's face showed her loneliness.

"Oh, Sarah, I'm sorry, I've made you want an answer mor'n ever," Cleota said.

"Don't apologize for your happiness. You deserve to be happy. You aren't responsible because I can't make up my mind. I've only got myself to blame. I think I'll slip away on Monday to visit my aunt in New Jersey."

"You tellin' your father?"

"He's going with me, but I'm not telling Clem and Samuel."

"It'll do 'em good to be on their own for a few days," Cleota added.

Sarah and her father drove away in the buggy at six the next morning. They boarded a train and chugged toward New Jersey.

The time together brought back old memories.

"Papa, do you remember when I used to dress up like a boy to go with you? My favorite place to go was the Arcadian Valley. I liked those times we rode out to look at Iron and Shepherd Mountains, or Pilot Knob. We climbed up on the highest point and looked- *forever*. I liked the Johnson Shut Ins and Elephant Rocks too. That was such a peaceful time for us. You got iron from there and sometimes loads of charcoal. You'd order what you needed and then we'd pick the goods up at Ste. Genevieve on the Mississippi. I miss those trips."

Her father squeezed her hand, "I missed those times too. I remember many things about our trips. I never left you home after your mother died. You don't know how much I missed you while you were in New Orleans. They wouldn't tell me where you were, but I did get comfort from the letters your contact passed to me. I wasn't able to travel for a time, so I had many hours to think, and feel."

"I'm sorry, but I just had to do something to catch the ones who hurt you and killed Daniel." She reached over to hug her father.

"I know you did. I understood that, but I still missed you," he said.

"If it hadn't been for Cleota, and the boys, I don't know what I would have done."

"They're good men. Gideon's a good boy too," he commented.

"He's much stronger than he used to be. When I first met him, he was sickly. I was afraid he wouldn't live, but it left him free to be my friend."

"I could tell that. You're all friends," he commented.

"Yes, that's part of the reason I wanted to go visit Aunt Louise."

"What's that?"

"Papa, I want to be married and have a family of my own. Both Clem and Samuel have asked me to marry them, but I can't decide which one I love the most." Sarah sighed.

Mr. Turner looked into his daughter's face. "You do have a problem there."

"What would you do, Papa?"

"I'm not about to give an opinion on that one. There's no way anyone can see into your heart. About as far as I can tell, either one would suit me for a son-in-law."

"I guess you can see my problem, they're both fine Christian men and I love them both."

"In what way?" he asked.

"Umh, like good brothers."

"Honey, you need a little more than that. I may be old, but I can remember that much," he said.

"Cleota says I need to have the shivers over someone to marry them."

"She does? Guess that's as good a description as any, but your head has to enter into it too," he said.

"Yes, he's got to be a believer." She thought a moment, "Daniel gave me the shivers."

She confessed, "Once in New Orleans, I knew some-one who might have given me the shivers, but my head had to reject him before it got that far." She didn't tell her father it was the man who caused Daniel's death.

"That's only using your good sense. That's what God gave you a brain for, and you've got a good one, common sense too," her father advised.

"I know, maybe my brain's too good for my heart, or the other way around."

"Hard to decipher that one," he smiled.

꿈ꞏ

Two weeks of idleness and shopping flew by with Aunt Louise. Goods had returned to the coastal shops. Sarah replenished her supplies of clothing and accessories, then purchased items for those left at home.

She caught herself thinking of both men. Today, her mind dwelt on Clem. *He's quiet and gentle. Sometimes Samuel is a bit flamboyant, frivolous? No, light-hearted. But that causes him to adjust easily. They both like Gideon and they treat Cleota and Moses well. They like my father. We all love each other, we are family.*

When Sarah returned to St. Louis at the end of the second week, Gideon was the first person Sarah looked for. Then her eyes sought Clem. His smile lighted her heart. Her gaze shifted to Samuel and his intense gaze unnerved her. It bought to memory the first time she received that gaze over a bolt of cloth in the Fuqua Store in New Orleans.

Did I shiver then? Maybe.

"Hello, boys. How are things going?"

"Fine with us, but Cleota's not feeling well. She went back to bed this morning. Gideon's been doing the cooking around here the last few days," Clem said.

"Oh, I'm sorry. I'll go see about her."

Sarah tapped two knuckles on Cleota's door. "May I come in?"

"Yes," came a muffled answer.

"The boys said you've been ill. Do I need to send for the doctor?" Sarah asked. She entered and closed the door softly.

"I hardly think this is a matter for the doctor," Cleota said.

"Are you sure?"

"Women been having babies since Adam and Eve. "In travail she shall bring forth children." I'm not at that stage yet, but I'm beginning."

"Cleota, you're with child?" Sarah asked.

"Sometimes, that's what happens to married folks," Cleota replied.

"You are happy about it, aren't you?"

"Very! Moses is beside himself, but he's afraid we're too old."

"Nonsense, God wouldn't have made us able to have babies into the forties if he didn't plan it that way." Sarah bustled around straightening covers. She dampened a cloth to place on Cleota's forehead.

Cleota removed it and wiped her face.

"I think I'd feel better if you'll help me freshen up a bit. Laying here feeling rumpled doesn't help me none," Cleota stated.

Sarah slid Cleota's gown up her arms and washed her hands to her elbows. "Sit up and I'll do your back."

"You don't need to."

"I know, but I want to. I love you Cleota. I want to take care of you and your baby just like you did when I was in need."

Sarah finished Cleota's back. She wrung out the washcloth. "Do you want to wash the rest of your body yourself?"

"Hand me the cloth."

"Would you like a fresh gown?" Sarah asked.

"Yes, there's one in the cabinet there."

Sarah changed her patient and settled her back into bed.

"I do feel fresher. Thank you Sarah, but I need to rest a minute." Cleota sank back into her freshly plumped pillow.

"Are you sure you're all right? I can get the doctor."

"If I'm not up in a couple of days, you can have him come. I should get over this before too many weeks."

"I don't know much, you'll have to tell me what to do for you."

Sarah turned to find Moses in the doorway, nervously turning his hat in his hands.

Sarah spoke to the couple, "We're back and ready to help you two out. Is there anything you need, Moses?"

"No Ma'am. I'd shor 'preciate it if you can help Cleota though," Moses said.

"I'll do my best. If there's nothing else, I'll go unpack."

Sarah turned to leave, but reassured the couple, "I'll be back in a bit and we'll see about dinner for you two. Take care of her Moses while I'm gone."

Three weeks later, Cleota's body began to adjust to her new status. As the sickness left, gradually she stirred from her room.

Sarah spoke of their plans, "Partners, we're partners, you give us the brains and help with the lighter duties." She continued, "We'll do the heavy things. How about that?"

"That will be fine. I'm sorry, I didn't think about getting so sick on you," Cleota replied.

"Don't apologize those are things we never know until they happen. Who knows, someday you may have to take care of me in the same situation."

Cleota's head snapped around. "Did you make up your mind while you were away?"

"Not really." Sarah sighed, "I'm leaning again, but who knows if I'll fall or not."

≈

Six weeks later, Sarah looked pensive. "Cleota, the parties didn't work. They were polite, but neither of them paid any attention to the other women. I've decided I am going to lock myself in my room to fast and pray for the next two days. Keep our family away, I've got to find an answer or go crazy trying."

Cleota cautioned the family at the dinner table when they asked for Sarah, "She has a decision to make and she's seeking the Lord's help. Leave her alone. When she's ready, she'll be out to give us her answer."

"Are you sure, she's not sick, maybe she caught what you had?" Clem commented.

"Hardly think so," Cleota replied.

"I'll volunteer to check on her for you," Samuel added.

"No, you boys run on. Give her time, that's what she needs now," Cleota directed.

≈

Sarah lay on her face in her bed. "Please Lord, give me a sign, help me make up my mind. This has gone on long enough. We're all getting impatient." She flopped to her stomach.

'The parties didn't help a bit, neither left me, unless I made them. I can't expect them to wait forever, it's not fair to any one."

Sarah drifted off to sleep. She drifted into nightmares.

In her distress, she dreamed she was drowning. Clem came to her rescue. When they reached dry land, Samuel gave her his coat to warm her.

Sarah awakened, cold and shivering. She pulled the quilt to her chin and curled into its warmth. She drifted away into their church during a wedding ceremony. She found herself walking down the aisle, but she could not see the face of her groom. She walked nearer and nearer. The man who awaited her turned, she saw the face of Clem, and the eyes of Samuel. The groom's head was covered with Clem's lighter hair.

Sarah awoke with tears streaming down her face. Her pillow already damp.

"Lord, I need an answer. Please give me a sign that is clear. All this is mixed. I'm not any nearer than I was when I started twenty-four hours ago. Am I to look elsewhere? Are you giving me the message that I can't make a decision between these two men?"

She prayed and prayed. Then she cried and prayed more.

Her turmoil continued through the long night.

Finally, her decision made, she slept peacefully and soundly for the next twelve hours.

ॐ

When Sarah came from her room, the first person she saw was Samuel. Her heart lurched and she motioned to him.

"I need to speak with you. Could you go for a walk with me?" she asked.

He had a surprised, but hopeful look on his face. "Let's go!"

Outside, she turned to look into his face, "Samuel, I've been attracted to you from the day I first met you. Your eyes have haunted me— you're the kind of man that can turn a woman's heart."

"But— ?"

Sarah bowed her head and took a deep breath.

"You know me too well."

She looked into his face, "Yes, I love you like a very dear brother. This is nothing against you, you are the dearest friend that anyone could ever have or ask for. I've prayed, but through all our getting to know each other better, I see how much Clem and I think alike, how much our goals are the same. We probably have a few things to work out, but I feel he is God's choice for me, and eventually, we'll be married— That is-   Clem and the Lord willing."

"I love you Sarah, I want only the best for you. Anything that makes you happy will please me," Samuel said.

"I know, I love you too," her eyes brimmed over.

"But, not in the way I want."

"I guess that's right, but don't give up— you'll find the one that's right for you. The Lord will provide."

"He always has. But I want you to remember one thing," Samuel reached for Sarah's hand.

"What's that?"

"If something happens and you don't get together with Clem. Will you let me know?"

"Would that be fair?" she asked.

"I say it would."

"No, I think it would be best if you didn't hold out hopes for you and me."

"You believe in killing a fellow, don't you?"

"I don't mean to be cruel, but no use suffering along in a slow death. Papa always said, *a quick death was more merciful.*"

"Your papa's usually right. I've come to realize that since we've lived with him."

"I've found him to usually be correct."

"If that's your last word, I'll be on my way. I've got a country to see, but I'll drop by once in a while to check up on you and ole Clem."

"I'd like that. You're the best brother I ever had."

"Come here," Samuel opened his arms to the slight figure before him. Sarah walked into his embrace. After a bear hug, he held her at arms length and studied her face. His eyes changed, he gave a sad smile.

His voice roughened, "I'm not accustomed to losing battles, but I'll concede on this one. Be happy, Sarah! That will be my prayer for you."

"I will be. Samuel. I've got that same prayer for you." Another tear overflowed and made a shiny line down her cheek.

Samuel wiped it away with his thumb. He clutched her to his chest and choked out, "Be— happy." He released her, but held onto her hand.

"Thanks, Samuel. My prayers will go with you."

"I know they will. Tell Clem, so long, for me. The others too.""

Sarah didn't trust her voice. She nodded and released Samuel's outstretched hand. He strolled to his horse.

Sarah stood alone. She watched him outfit the animal and gather his reins. He swung aboard.

Samuel rode away, but before he turned the corner, he looked back at Sarah. She tentatively raised her hand in farewell.

His hand went up in a decisive sweep.

"So long. Take care of yourself." He heeled his horse into a lope and turned out of sight.

Sarah sank into the porch swing and sobbed broken-heartedly.

Clem paced the floor inside the house.

After an hour, Sarah's father took pity on him. "I heard Samuel leave a long time ago. Go on out, Son. I think she'll be ready to talk to you now."

"Sir, do you know something I should know?"

"I think it's her place to tell you."

Clem could stand to wait no longer. He came out on the porch to find Sarah with her feet drawn up in the swing. Her face rested on her knees.

He walked softly to face her. He could see an occasional gasp, as she recovered from her sobs.

Like an injured child, went through his mind. He reached out a tentative and trembling hand in comfort.

"Sarah, are you all right?"

She leaped to her feet.

Startled, he stepped back, but in one step, she clutched him to herself. Her face was wet. He could not determine the problem.

He bristled, "Sarah, did Samuel hurt you?"

"No— I hurt him," she sobbed.

Attempting patience, he asked, "How did you do that?"

"I told him I couldn't marry him."

Clem hesitated, "If that's the way you feel, you had to tell him."

"That's what I thought, but it was so painful for him."

"Ole Sam is flexible, he'll recover. That's one good thing about him, he always lands on his feet."

"I know, but I do love him."

Clem had trouble talking around a lump in his throat. "I know you love him, but why did you tell him you wouldn't marry him?"

"Because— ," Sarah hiccuped, "I'm marrying you, if

you still want me."

Unbelieving, Clem unwound Sarah's arms from his waist and pushed her back so he could look into her face.

"What did you say?"

"I said that I'm marrying you, if— "

"That's what I thought you said."

Clem clasped Sarah close again and lifted her from her feet.

She threw back her head and gave him a radiant smile through her tears. He accepted the perfect opportunity to find her lips with his.

All the years of pent-up emotion flowed through both of them. Breathless, Clem planted Sarah's feet back on the porch floor. She leaned against him.

"You did it," she whispered.

"What?"

"You gave me the shivers."

"I like the sound of that, but what's it supposed to mean?" he asked.

"Cleota and Papa told me that if I was marrying someone, I ought to wait for the shivers."

"As opposed to?"

"Head— *brains*."

"I agree, with both criteria."

"Do I give you the shivers too?" Sarah asked.

"You certainly do, and *you have*, ever since I met you three years ago."

"You've certainly been a patient man!"

"Not on my own, the Lord helped me in that way," Clem replied.

"He didn't let me in on His plans for *us*, before. I thought I'd go crazy," she said.

"Well, neither of us has to be patient much longer," he squeezed her hand. "When can we marry?"

"She reached her hand to his face, "As soon as

possible."

He kissed her again. "Let's go tell our family.".

They turned and walked back into the house with their arms around each other. Their family waited expectantly in the sitting room, ready to celebrate an extended evening.

The End

#   #   #

About the Author and Cover Artist

Author, Anita L. Allee was born on a farm in Ralls County, Missouri, one of four children. She is married to a retired public school administrator and has two grown daughters and five grandchildren.

The author and Mary King Hayden, cover artist, were at the University of Missouri, Columbia, during the same years and both hold BS degrees in Education. Both are retired public school teachers and professional volunteers, being involved in multiple community and church activities in their present hometown of Versailles, MO.

Anita is available for speaking engagements with adults and students. She has gone to a number of schools and organizations with experiential or writing information.

Anita L. Allee, 13216 Church Road, Versailles, MO 65084
e-mail: anviallee@earthlink.net